The Philadelphia Story

A COMEDY IN THREE ACTS

By Philip Barry

SAMUEL FRENCH, INC.

45 WEST 25TH STREET   NEW YORK 10010
7623 SUNSET BOULEVARD   HOLLYWOOD 90046
LONDON   *TORONTO*

THE PHILADELPHIA STORY

STORY OF THE PLAY

Tracy Lord, of the Philadelphia Lords, has married C. K. Dexter Haven and divorced him when he, resenting her chilling attitude toward the comforting virtues of domesticity, takes to liquor. A little while later she has taken up with a handsome snob of the mines named Kittredge and is about to marry him. One of the calender paper social gossip weeklies sends a reporter and a camera woman to cover the wedding. They are injected into the house by Tracy's brother, who hopes to divert their attention from Father Lord's affair with a Broadway actress. Tracy, already a little shaken in her urge for Kittredge, finds herself suddenly bowled over by Connor, the fascinating reporter. At the end of a pre-wedding party, at which the champagne flows like ginger ale, she and Connor go for a dip in the pool. Tracy always had been an uncertain champagne drinker. The last time she drank a lot of it she went out on the roof to salute the moon. Now the wedding is threatened. Kittredge takes his frock coat and goes home.

Copy of program of the first performance of "The Philadelphia Story" as produced at the Shubert Theatre, New York:

The Theatre Guild, Inc.

presents

THE PHILADELPHIA STORY

A new comedy by Philip Barry

Directed by Robert D. Sinclair

Designed and lighted by Robert Edmond Jones

Production under the supervision of
Theresa Helburn and Lawrence Langer

CHARACTERS

TRACY LORD .... *Katherine Hepburn*
DINAH LORD .... *Lenore Lonergan*
MARGARET LORD .... *Vera Allen*
ALEXANDER (SANDY) LORD .... *Dan Tobin*
THOMAS .... *Owen Coll*
WILLIAM (UNCLE WILLIE) TRACY....*Forrest Orr*
ELIZABETH (LIZ) IMBRIE...........*Shirley Booth*
MACAULAY (MIKE) CONNOR.........*Van Heflin*
GEORGE KITTREDGE .... *Frank Fenton*
C. K. DEXTER HAVEN..............*Joseph Cotton*
SETH LORD .... *Nicholas Joy*
ELSIE .... *Lorraine Bate*
MAC .... *Hayden Rorke*
MAY .... *Myrtle Tannehill*
EDWARD .... *Philip Foster*

Stage Manager—Karl Nielsen

Asst. Stage Manager—Hayden Rorke

5

ACTION AND SCENE

The action of the play takes place in the course of twenty-four hours at the Seth Lords' house in the country near Philadelphia.

The time is late June of the present year, and the Scenes are as follows:

ACT ONE: *The sitting room. Late morning, Friday.*

ACT II:
SCENE I: *The porch. Late evening, Friday.*

SCENE II: *The porch. Early morning, Saturday.*

ACT III: *The sitting-room. Late morning, Saturday.*

DESCRIPTION OF CHARACTERS

DINAH *is all of fifteen years old.*
TRACY *is a strikingly lovely girl of twenty-four.*
MARGARET LORD, *their mother, is a young and smart
  forty-seven.*
SANDY LORD: *Twenty-six.*
UNCLE WILLIE TRACY: *Sixty-two.*
MIKE CONNOR: *Thirty.*
LIZ IMBRIE: *Twenty-eight.*
MAC: *The night watchman, about thirty.*
GEORGE KITTREDGE: *Aged thirty-two.*
DEXTER: *Twenty-eight. Pleasant and good-looking.*
SETH: *Tall, handsome, suave. Fifty.*

The Philadelphia Story

ACT ONE

*The sitting room of the Lords' house in the country
near Philadelphia is a large, comfortably fur-
nished room of a somewhat faded elegance con-
taining a number of very good Victorian pieces.
The entrance from the hall is at Right 2 upstage, down two broad, shallow steps. The entrance into what the family still call "the parlor"
is through double doors downstage Right 1. At
Left are two glass doors leading to the porch. A
writing desk stands between them. There is a
large marble fireplace in back wall with chairs
Right and Left of it; a stool in front of it. A
grand piano in the corner at up Left. Chairs and
a table are at down Left Center, and at down
Right Center, a coffee table, an easy chair and
a sofa. There is a large and fine portrait over
the fireplace and other paintings here and there.
A wall cabinet Right of fireplace contains a
quantity of bric-a-brac and there is more of it,
together with a number of signed photographs
in silver frames, upon the tables and piano. A
bookcase above doors Right 1. There are also
several cardboard boxes strewn about, indicat-
ing an approaching wedding.*

It is late on a Friday morning in June, on

9

overcast day. DINAH, *who is all of fifteen years old, is stretched out on the sofa reading a set of printer's galley proofs.* TRACY, *a strikingly lovely girl of twenty-four, sits in the chair at Left, a leather writing set upon her knees, scribbling notes. She wears slacks and a blouse.* MARGARET LORD, *their mother, a young and smart forty-seven, comes in from the hall with three more boxes in her arms. She places them upon the table near* TRACY.

AT RISE: DINAH, *fifteen, is stretched out on the sofa, over Right, reading three proof-sheets while* TRACY, *twenty-four, is in the armchair Left of the table over Left, writing "Thank-you" notes. She has a leather portfolio in her lap.* MARGARET, *forty-seven, enters at rise.*

MARGARET. *(Entering Right 1 with three boxes. Going to back of table Left)* I'm so terribly afraid that some of the cards for these last-minute presents must have got mixed. Look at them, Tracy—perhaps you can tell. *(Puts boxes upper end of table.)*

TRACY. In a minute, Mother. I'm up to my neck in these blank thank-you notes.

DINAH. *(Rises)* This stinks! *(Goes in Center with papers.)*

MARGARET. *(Back of table)* Don't say "stinks," darling. If absolutely necessary, "smells"—but only if absolutely necessary. What is it? *(Crosses to desk —picks up three-page typed list.)*

DINAH. *(Going up to piano)* I found it in Sandy's room. It's something that's going to be in a magazine. It certainly stinks all right.

MARGARET. *(At desk)* Keep out of your brother's things, dear—and his house. *(Crossing down Left, reading)* Ninety-four for the ceremony, five hundred and six for the reception—I don't know where we'll put them all, if it should rain. *(Looks out Left 1.)*

DINAH. *(Crossing down back of table Left)* It won't rain.

MARGARET. *(Crossing below table to chair Left Center; sits)* Uncle Willie wanted to insure against it with Lloyd's but I wouldn't let him. If I was God and someone bet I wouldn't let it rain, I'd show him fast enough. This second page is solid Cadwalader. Twenty-six.

DINAH. *(Back of table)* That's a lot of Cadwalader.

MARGARET. One, my child, is a lot of Cadwalader.

TRACY. How do you spell omelet?

MARGARET. O-m-m-e-l-e-t.

TRACY. I thought there was another "l."

(DINAH *moves up to and leans on piano, reading proof-sheets.)*

MARGARET. The omelet dish from the—? *(Rises.)*

TRACY. You said it was an omelet dish.

MARGARET. It might be for fish.

TRACY. Fish dish? That sounds idiotic. *(Tears up card—starts new letter.)*

MARGARET. I should simply say "Thank you so much for your lovely silver dish."

TRACY. *(Taking up card from another box)* Here's the tag, "Old Dutch Muffin Ear, Cirea 1810"— What the— *(Dropping card)* I am simply enchanted with your old Dutch Muffin Ear—with which my husband and I will certainly hear any muffin coming a mile away.

DINAH. *(Crossing down back of table)* Lookit, Tracy: don't you think you've done enough notes for one day? *(Starts to handle things on table.)*

TRACY. *(Waving her off)* Don't disturb me. *(Picking up cards, reads)* From Cousin Horace Ma··

comber, one pair of game shears, looking like hell. *(Picks up shears.)*

DINAH. He's so awful. What did he send the other time?

TRACY. *(Writing "game shears" on the card)* No one to speak of sent anything the other time.

MARGARET. *(In armchair)* It's such a pity your brother Junius can't be here for your wedding. London's so far away.

DINAH. *(Back of table)* I miss old Junius: you did a good job when you had him, Mother.

MARGARET. The first is always the best. They deteriorate as you go on.

(A look between DINAH and TRACY.)

TRACY. *(Writes note)* There was no occasion to send anything the other time.

DINAH. *(Reading the proof sheets—crossing to Center)* This is certainly pretty rooty-tooty all right.

TRACY. *(Still writing at table)* It would scarcely be considered a wedding at all, the other time. When you run off to Maryland on a sudden impulse—as Dexter and I did—

DINAH. *(Crossing back behind table Left)* Ten months is quite long to be married, though. You can have a baby in nine, can't you?

TRACY. I guess, if you put your mind to it.

DINAH. Why didn't you?

TRACY. *(Looks up from her writing)* Mother, don't you think it's time for her nap?

DINAH. I imagine you and George'll have slews of 'em. *(Slouches to Center.)*

TRACY. I hope so, all like you, dear, with the same wild grace.

(DINAH stops Center and looks at her. TRACY rises; picks up box of envelopes and places on desk.)

DINAH. *(Center)* Lookit: "the other time"—he's back from wherever he's been.

(TRACY *goes in to back of table Left.)*

MARGARET. *(After a glance at* TRACY*)* What do you mean?

DINAH. Dexter, of course. I saw his car in front of his house: *(Crossing Right)* the roadster. It must be him.

MARGARET. When? When did you?

DINAH. *(At sofa)* This morning, early, when I was out exercising The Hoofer. *(Sits on sofa Right; puts sheets on coffee table.)*

MARGARET. Why didn't you tell us?

TRACY. *(Back of table, near* MARGARET's *chair)* I'm not worried, Mother. The only trouble Mr. C. K. Dexter Haven ever gave me was when he married me.—*You* might say the same for one Seth Lord. If you'd just face it squarely as I did— *(Sits on end of table.)*

MARGARET. That will do! I will allow none of you to criticise your father.

TRACY. What are we expected to do when he treats you—

MARGARET. Did you hear me, Tracy?

TRACY. *(Rising)* All right, I give up.

MARGARET. *(Softly, and taking* TRACY's *hand)* —And in view of this second attempt of yours, it might pay you to remind yourself that neither of us has proved to be a very great success as a wife.

TRACY. *(Crossing to behind table)* We just picked the wrong first husbands, that's all.

MARGARET. That's an extremely vulgar remark.

TRACY. Oh, who cares about either of them any more— *(Crosses back of* MARGARET, *who is in chair Left Center. Crouches to embrace her)* Golly Moses, I'm going to be happy now.

MARGARET. Darling.

TRACY. Isn't George an angel?

MARGARET. George is an angel.

TRACY. Is he handsome, or is he not?

MARGARET. George is handsome.

TRACY. *(Straightens up and picks up boxes from table, also writing-case)* Suds. I'm a lucky girl. *(Crosses Right upper.)*

DINAH. I like Dexter.

TRACY. *(Continuing on her way up Right)* Really? Why don't you ask him to lunch, or something? *(Goes out Right 2.)*

DINAH. *(Looking after her for a moment—rises and crosses to Center)* She's awfully mean about him, isn't she?

MARGARET. He was rather mean to her, my dear.

DINAH. *(Over Left Center at MARGARET'S chair)* Did he really sock her?

MARGARET. *(Still comparing lists and letters)* Don't say "sock," darling. "Strike" is quite an ugly enough word.

DINAH. But did he really?

MARGARET. I'm afraid I don't know the details.

DINAH. *(By MARGARET at chair Left Center)* Cruelty and drunkenness, it said.

MARGARET. Dinah!

DINAH. It was right in the papers.

MARGARET. You read too much. You'll spoil your eyes.

DINAH. *(Crossing Right to sofa)* I think it's an awful thing to say about a man. I don't think they like things like that said about them.

MARGARET. I'm sure they don't.

DINAH. *(At sofa picks up three proof sheets)* Father's going to be hopping when he reads all this about himself in that magazine, *Destiny,* when it comes out.

MARGARET. All what? *About whom? (Turns to face DINAH.)*

DINAH. Father,—that they're going to publish.

MARGARET. Dinah, what *are* you talking about?

DINAH. *(Crossing Center with paper)* It's what they call proof sheets for some article they're going to call, "Broadway and Finance," and Father's in it, and so they just sent it on to Sandy—sort of—you know, on approval. *(Crosses Left Center.)*

MARGARET. But the article! What does the article say? *(Takes paper from her.)*

DINAH. Oh, it's partly about Father backing three shows for that dancer—what's her name— Tina Mara—and his early history—and about the stables—and why he's living in New York, instead of with us, any more, and—

MARGARET. Great heaven—what on earth can we do?

DINAH. Couldn't Father sue them for liable?

MARGARET. But it's true—it's all— *(Realizing her error, she glances at DINAH, then rises and crosses to Right at coffee table)* That is, I mean to say— *(Reading sheets.)*

DINAH. I don't think the part about Tina Mara is, the way they put it. It's simply full of innundo. *(Sits in armchair Left Center.)*

MARGARET. *(Turning)* Of what?

DINAH. Of innundo. *(Rests elbow on table Left)* Oh, I do wish something would happen here. Nothing ever possibly in the least ever happens. *(Rises, crossing Right)* Next year can I go to the Conservatory in New York? They teach you to sing and dance and act and everything at once. Can I, Mother?

MARGARET. *(Front of sofa, down Right)* Save your dramatics, Dinah. Oh, why didn't Sandy *tell* me!

DINAH. Mother, why won't Tracy *ask* her own *father* to her *wedding?*

MARGARET. *(Crossing over Left to the table— picks up list and three letters which she had left there)* Your sister has very definite opinions about certain things.

DINAH. *(Crosses to Left Center to* MARGARET*)* She's sort of—you know—hard, isn't she?

MARGARET. Not hard—none of my children is that, I hope. Tracy sets exceptionally high standards for herself, that's all, and although she lives up to them, other people aren't always quite able to. If your Uncle Willie Tracy comes in, tell him to wait. I want to see him. *(Starts for window Left 1.)*

DINAH. *(Follows her to Left)* Tell me one thing: don't you think it's stinking not at least to *want* Father?

MARGARET. *(Turning to her)* Yes, darling, between ourselves I think it's good and stinking. *(Goes out Left 1.)*

DINAH. And I bet if Dexter knew what she— *(*DINAH *waits a moment, then goes to the telephone on desk and dials four numbers)* Hello. May I please speak to Mr. Dexter Haven—what?—Dexter! It's you! *(Then affectedly)* A very great pleasure to have you back. Dinah, you goat, Dinah Lord. What?—You bet!—Lookit, Dexter, Tracy says why don't you come right over for lunch? What? But she told me to ask you.—Listen, though, maybe it would be better if you'd— Hello!—Hello! *(Taps the telephone several times to get operator. Hangs up as* TRACY *enters Right 1 with a large roll of parchment.)*

TRACY. *(Entering, crossing to Left)* Who was that?

DINAH. Wrong number.

(TRACY *moves over Left to back of table.* DINAH *moves to her.)*

TRACY. *(Spreads roll of paper out on table)* Listen, darling, give me a hand with this cockeyed seating arrangement, will you? At least hold it down.—George doesn't want the Grants at the bridal table. (SANDY LORD, *twenty-six, comes in from Right 2)* He says they're fast. He—

SANDY. *(Entering and going down Center)* Hello, kids.

TRACY. *(Rushes up Center to embrace him)* Sandy!

SANDY. Where's Mother?

(DINAH *crosses Left Center back of armchair.)*

TRACY. She's around. How's New York?—How's Sue?—How's the baby?

SANDY. Blooming. They sent their love, sorry they can't make the wedding. Is there a party tonight, of course?

TRACY. Aunt Geneva's throwing a monster.

SANDY. Boy, am I going to get plastered. *(Crossing to armchair L. to DINAH)* Hello, little fellah. *(Makes a boxing pass at her.)*

DINAH. Hello, yourself.

SANDY. *(Giving her a flat box)* This is for you, Mug; get the three race-horses into the paddock. It's tough. Work it out.

DINAH. Oh, thanks. *(Remains at Left Center armchair.)*

SANDY. *(Turning to TRACY)* Sue's and my wedding present comes by registered mail, Tracy—and a pretty penny it set me back.

TRACY. You're a bonny boy, Sandy. I love you.

SANDY. Mutual—

(TRACY *goes to Left armchair; looks at toy with* DINAH.*)*

MARGARET. *(Re-enters Left 1. She carries three envelopes and the three proof sheets. As she enters)* I was wondering about you.

SANDY. *(Crosses Left below table—kisses her)* Give us a kiss.—You look fine.—Imagine this, a grandmother. How's everything? *(Goes to front of table.)*

MARGARET. *(Left of Left table)* Absolute chaos.

SANDY. *(Front of table Left)* Just how you like it, eh? Just when you function best!

MARGARET. How's my precious grandchild?

SANDY. Couldn't be better; Sue too. Ten more days in the hospital, and back home they'll be.

MARGARET. *(Crossing Right below him to sofa with papers)* I broke into your house and did up the nursery.

SANDY. *(Crossing Center)* Good girl. Where's George, Tracy?

TRACY. *(Sitting on arm of chair Right)* He's staying in the Gatehouse. He still had business things to clear up and I thought he'd be quieter there.

SANDY. *(Crosses below table to Right Center)* Did he see his picture in *Dime?* Was he sore at the "Former Coal Miner" caption?

MARGARET. *(At sofa)* What about this absurd article about your father and—er—Tina Mara in *Destiny?* Can't it be stopped?

(DINAH *goes in Center.*)

TRACY. *(Rises, crossing Right)* About Father and —let me see! *(Takes article from MARGARET.)*

SANDY. Where'd you get hold of that? *(Tries to take it from her.)*

MARGARET. *(Sits sofa)* Get ready for lunch, Dinah.

DINAH. *(Going up Right, sits on step—works at puzzle)* In a minute. I'm busy.

TRACY. *(Reading sheets)* Oh! The absolute devils— Who publishes *Destiny? (Sits on armchair Right.)*

SANDY. *(Center)* Sidney Kidd.—Also *Dime,* also *Spy,* the picture sheet. I worked on *Dime* for two summers, you know that.

TRACY. Stopped? It's got to be! I'll go to him myself.

SANDY. *(Center)* A fat lot of good that would do. You're too much alike. God save us from the strong. *(Crossing to behind armchair Right Center)* I saw Kidd the day before yesterday. It took about three hours, but I finally got through to him.

TRACY. What happened?

SANDY. I think I fixed things.

TRACY. How?

SANDY. That would be telling.

MARGARET. Just so long as your father never hears of it.

SANDY. I had a copy of the piece made, and sent it around to his flat, with a little note saying, "How do you like it?"

TRACY. You are a fellah.

MARGARET. Sandy!

SANDY. Why not? Let him worry a little.

(THOMAS *enters Right 2; comes down steps.)*

TRACY. Let him worry a lot!

SANDY. *(Crosses up to him)* Yes, Thomas?

THOMAS. *(At door)* Mr. Connor and the lady say they will be down directly, sir.

SANDY. Thanks, that's fine. Tell May or Elsie to look after Miss Imbrie, will you?

THOMAS. Very good, sir. *(Goes out Right 2.)*

MARGARET. What's all this?

TRACY. "Mr. Connor and—?"

SANDY. *(Takes paper from TRACY; crossing Left*

Center, sits on arm of chair) Mike Connor—Macaulay Connor, his name is.—And—er—Elizabeth Imbrie. I'm putting them up for over the wedding. They're quite nice. You'll like them.

TRACY. You asked people to stay in this house without even asking us?

MARGARET. I think it's very queer indeed.

TRACY. I think it's queerer than that—*I* think it's paranoic! *(Rises and crosses Left Center to him.)*

SANDY. Keep your shirt on.—I just sort of drifted into them and we sort of got to talking about what riots weddings are as a rule, and they'd never been to a Philadelphia one, and—

TRACY. You're lying, Sandy.—I can always tell.

SANDY. Now look here, Tracy—

TRACY. Look where? "Elizabeth Imbrie"—I know that name! She's a—wait—damn your eyes, Sandy, she's a photographer!

SANDY. For a fact?

TRACY. For a couple of facts—and a famous one!

SANDY. Well, it might be nice to have some good shots of the wedding.

TRACY. What are they doing here?

SANDY. Just now I suppose they're brushing up and going to the bathroom. *(Rising, Right Center)* They're very interesting people. She's practically an artist, and he's written a couple of books—and—and I thought you liked interesting people.

DINAH. *(Rising) I* do.

(SANDY crosses to Right armchair. DINAH is up on step up Right.)

TRACY. I know—now I know! They're from *Destiny—Destiny* sent them!

MARGARET. *Destiny?*

SANDY. *(Sitting in armchair Right)* You're just a mass of intuition, Tracy.

TRACY. Well, they can go right back again. *(Goes to him.)*

SANDY. No, they can't. Not till they get their story.

TRACY. Story? What story?

SANDY. The Philadelphia story.

MARGARET. And what on earth's that?

SANDY. Well, it seems Kidd has had Connor and Imbrie and a couple of others down here for two months doing the town: I mean writing it up. It's to come out in three parts in the Autumn. "Industrial Philadelphia," "Historical Philadelphia"—and then the third—

TRACY. I'm going to be sick.

SANDY. Yes, dear, "Fashionable Philadelphia."

TRACY. I *am* sick. *(Turns to Center.)*

MARGARET. But why us? Surely there are other families who—

TRACY. *(Crossing a bit to Left Center)* Yes—why not the Drexels or Biddles or the *qu'est-qu-c'est* Cassats?

SANDY. *(Seated)* We go even further back: It's those Quakers.—And of course there's your former marriage and your looks and your general prowess in golf and fox-hunting, with a little big game on the side, and your impending second marriage into the coal-fields—

TRACY. *(Center)* Never mind that!

SANDY. I don't, but they do. It's news, darling, news.

MARGARET. Is there no such thing as privacy any more?

TRACY. Only in bed, Mother, and not always there.

SANDY. Anyhow I thought I was licked—and what else could I do?

TRACY. A trade, eh? So we're to let them publish

the inside story of my wedding in order to keep Father's wretched little affair quiet!

MARGARET. It's utterly and completely disgusting.

SANDY. It was my suggestion, not Kidd's. I may have been put in the way of making it. I don't know. It's hard to tell with the future President of the United States.

TRACY. What's the writer's name again?

SANDY. Connor, Macaulay Connor. I don't think he likes the assignment any more than we do—the gal either. They were handling the Industrial end.

TRACY. *(Crossing to desk to phone—dials four numbers)* My heart's breaking for them.

MARGARET. *(Rises)* I don't know what the world is coming to. It's an absolute invasion; two strange people tramping through the house, prying and investigating—

TRACY. *(At the telephone)* Maybe we're going through a revolution without knowing it. *(In telephone)* Hello, is Mr. Briggs there?—This is Tracy Lord, Mr. Briggs.—Look, I wonder if you happen to have on hand any books by Macaulay Connor? (SANDY *rises*) You have!—Could you surely send them out this afternoon?—Thanks, Mr. Briggs, you're sweet. *(Hangs up.* SANDY *goes in Left Center)* —If they've got to have a story, I'll give them a story— I'll give them one they can't get through the mails!

SANDY. *(Left Center)* Oh—oh—I was afraid of this—

TRACY. Who the hell do they think they are, barging in on peaceful people—watching every little mannerism—jotting down notes on how we sit, and stand, and talk, and eat and move—

DINAH. *(Crossing down back of sofa)* Will they do that?

TRACY. *(Center)* —And all in the horrible snide corkscrew English!—Well, if we have to submit to it to save Father's face—which incidentally doesn't deserve it—I'm for giving them a picture of home life that will stand their hair on end.

MARGARET. *(Right)* You will do nothing of the sort, Tracy. *(Sits sofa.)*

SANDY. *(Left, embracing* TRACY*)* She thinks she'll be the outrageous Miss Lord. The fact is, she'll probably be Sweetness and Light to the neck.

TRACY. Oh, will I? *(Turns out of his arm, to back of armchair Right.)*

SANDY. You don't know yet what being under the microscope does to people. I felt it a little coming out in the car. It's a funny feeling.

MARGARET. It's odd how self-conscious we've all become over the worldly possessions that once made us so confident.

SANDY. *(Center)* I know; you catch yourself explaining away your dough, the way you would a black eye: you've just run into it in the dark or something.

MARGARET. We shall be ourselves with them; very much ourselves.

DINAH. *(Back of sofa)* But Mother, you want us to create a good impression, don't you?

MARGARET. *(To* SANDY*)* They don't know that *we* know what they're here for, I hope?

(TRACY *sits on the arm upper end of sofa.***)**

SANDY. No; that was understood.

DINAH. *(Crossing down lower end of sofa)* I should think it would look awfully funny to them, Father's not being here for his own daughter's wedding.

TRACY. Would you now?

SANDY. That's all right; I fixed that, too. *(Goes in Right Center back of armchair.)*

TRACY. How do you mean you did?

SANDY. I told Sue to send a telegram before dinner. "Confined to bed with a cold, unable to attend nuptials, oceans of love, Father."

MARGARET. Not just in those words!

SANDY. Not exactly.—It'll come on the telephone and Thomas will take it and you won't have your glasses and he'll read it aloud to you.

MARGARET. Tracy, will you promise to behave like a lady, if only for my sake?

TRACY. I'll do my best, Mrs. Lord. I don't know how good that is.

MARGARET. Go put a dress on.

TRACY. Yes, Mother.

MARGARET. *(Rises)* There are too many legs around here.

TRACY. *(Rises)* Suds! I'll be pure Victorian, all frills and ruffles, conversationally chaste as an egg. (UNCLE WILLIE TRACY, *sixty-two, comes in from the Right 1 door)* Hello, Uncle Willie. Where did you come from? *(Gets back of table Left for roll of paper.)*

UNCLE WILLIE. *(Down Right)* Your Great-aunt Geneva has requested my absence from the house until dinner time. Can you give me lunch, Margaret?

MARGARET. But of course! With pleasure—

DINAH. Hello, Uncle Willie— *(She goes up— leaves toy on bookcase and stops behind armchair Right Center.)*

SANDY. How are you, Uncle Willie?

WILLIE. Alexander and Dinah, good morning. *(Crossing Center)* My esteemed wife, the old warhorse, is certainly spreading herself for your party. *I* seriously question the propriety of (TRACY *goes down Center)* any such display in such times. But she— Why aren't you being married in church, Tracy?

TRACY. *(At Left Center chair)* I like the parlor

here so much better. Didn't you think it looked pretty as you came through?

UNCLE WILLIE. That is not the point. The point is that I've sunk thousands in that church, and I'd like to get some use of it.—Give me a glass of sherry, Margaret. *(Goes in Center.)*

(DINAH *goes down* L.C. TRACY *goes to* SANDY, *back of Right Center armchair.)*

MARGARET. Not until lunch time, my dear.

UNCLE WILLIE. These women.

DINAH. *(At Left Center)* You're really a wicked old man, aren't you?

UNCLE WILLIE. *(Points to the porch Left)* What's that out there?

(DINAH *turns to look. He vigorously pinches her behind.)*

DINAH. Ouch!

(SANDY, *standing at upper end of sofa, is chatting with* TRACY.)

UNCLE WILLIE. Never play with fire, child. *(Looks at the* OTHERS *over Right)* What's a-lack here? What's a-stirrin'? What's amiss?

SANDY. Uncle Willie, do you know anything about the laws of libel?

UNCLE WILLIE. *(Sitting in Right armchair)* Certainly I know about the laws of libel. Why shouldn't I? I know all about them. In 1916, I, Willie Q. Tracy, successfully defended the *Post,* and George Lorimer personally, against one of the cleverest, one of the subtlest—why? What do you want to say?

SANDY. *(Sits on sofa)* It isn't what *I* want to say—

TRACY. *(Breaking in—sits at his feet on floor Center)* Is it enough if they can simply prove that it is true?

(DINAH goes back of him; sits on arm of sofa.)

UNCLE WILLIE. *(Turns to* TRACY*)* Certainly not! Take me; if I was totally bald and wore a toupee, if I had flat feet, with these damnable metal arches, false teeth, and a case of double—

DINAH. Poor Uncle Willie.

UNCLE WILLIE. I said *"If* I had." *(*DINAH*, behind him, leans over and gives a derisive laugh through "haw")* —And if such— *(*WILLIE *gives her a dirty look)* —facts were presented in the public prints in such a manner as to hold me up to public ridicule, I could collect substantial damages,—and would, if it took me all winter.

TRACY. *(Rising)* Suppose the other way around; suppose they printed things that weren't true.

UNCLE WILLIE. *(Rising and crossing Center.* TRACY *sits on arm of chair Right Center)* Suppose they did? Suppose it was erroneously stated, that during my travels as a young man I was married in a native ceremony to a dusky maiden in British Guinea, I doubt if I could collect a cent. *(Looks off up Right 2—clears throat—crossing up)* Who are these two strange people coming down the hall?

(The FAMILY *rises, frozen in their tracks a second.)*

MARGARET. *(Rises)* Oh, good gracious!

(DINAH goes up to doorway Right 2.)

TRACY. Come on—out. *(Goes Center, grabs* WILLIE *and leads him to down Right)* What was she like, Uncle Willie?

(SANDY *gets in corner up Right near mantel.*)

WILLIE. Who?

TRACY. (*Crossing Right*) British Guinea?

WILLIE. (*Crossing Right*) So very unlike your Aunt Geneva, my dear. (*And they exit Right 1.*)

MARGARET. (*Crossing up for* DINAH—*takes hold of her—moves down Right with her*) Dinah—

DINAH. But, Mother, oughtn't we—?

MARGARET. Sandy can entertain them until we—until we collect ourselves. (*Puts* DINAH *out Right 1.*)

SANDY. (*Crossing to* MARGARET *at door Right 1*) What'll I say?

MARGARET. I wish I could tell you—in a few very well-chosen words. (*She goes out.*)

(SANDY *is alone for a moment; leans against bookcase, Right.* MIKE CONNOR, *thirty, and* LIZ IMBRIE, *twenty-eight, come in from the hall.* LIZ *has a small and important camera hanging from a leather strap around her neck.*)

LIZ. (*Enters from Right 2, crossing Left Center*) —In here?

MIKE. (*Entering down Center—gazes about room—notices crystal chandelier*) He said the sitting room. I suppose that's contrasted to the living room, the ballroom—the drawing room—the morning room—the— (*He sees* SANDY) Oh, hello again. Here you are.

(LIZ *goes over Left to Left of table and sits.*)

SANDY. Here I am. (*Goes Center.*)

MIKE. (*Up Center toward mantel*) It's quite a place.

SANDY. (*Crossing up to* MIKE) It is, isn't it?—I

couldn't help overhearing you as you came in. Do you mind if I say something?

MIKE. Not at all. What?

SANDY. Your approach to your job seems definitely antagonistic. I don't think it's fair. I think you ought to give us a break.

MIKE. It's not a job I asked for. *(Goes down Left Center.)*

SANDY. *(Up Right Center)* I know it's not. But in spite of it, and in spite of certain of our regrettable inherited characteristics, we just might be fairly decent. Why not wait and see?

MIKE. *(Sits Right of table Left)* You have quite a style yourself. (SANDY *picks up stool at fireplace, crossing down Center)* —You're on the *Saturday Evening Post,* did you say?

SANDY. I work for it.

MIKE. Which end?

SANDY. Editorial. *(Sits on stool he brought down.)*

MIKE. I have to tell you, in all honesty, that I'm opposed to everything you represent.

SANDY. *Destiny* is hardly a radical sheet: what is it you're doing—boring from within?

MIKE. —And I'm not a Communist, not by a long shot.

LIZ. Just a small pin-feather in the Left Wing. (MIKE *looks at her)* —Sorry.

SANDY. Jeffersonian Democrat?

MIKE. *(Looks at him)* That's more like it.

SANDY. Have you ever seen his house at Monticello? *It's* quite a place too.

LIZ. Home Team One; Visitors Nothing— *(Rises)* Is this house very old, Mr. Lord? *(Goes up Left.)*

SANDY. No, there are a very few old ones on the Main Line— The Gatehouse is, of course. Father's grandfather built that for a summer place when they all lived on Rittenhouse Square Father and

Mother did this about 1910—the spring before my brother Junius was born. He's the oldest. You won't meet him, he's in the diplomatic service in London.

MIKE. *(To* LIZ*)* Wouldn't you know? *(Putting out cigarette on table tray.)*

SANDY. *I* worked for Sidney Kidd once. What do you make of him?

MIKE. *(After a short pause)* A brilliant editor, and a very wonderful man. *(Gets cards from his pocket.)*

LIZ. Also, our bread and butter.

SANDY. Sorry to have been rude.

MIKE. *(Looking through cards)* I suppose you're all of you opposed to the Administration?

SANDY. The present one? No—as a matter of fact we're Loyalists.

MIKE. *(Has a sheaf of typewritten cards and looks at them)* Surprise, surprise..—The Research Department didn't give us much data.—Your sister's fiancé—George Kittredge—aged thirty-two.—Since last year General Manager Quaker State Coal, in charge of operation.—Is that right?

SANDY. That's right.—And brilliant at it.

MIKE. So I've heard tell. I seem to have read about him first back in '35 or '36.—Up from the bottom, wasn't he?

*(*LIZ *sits on arm of Left Center chair.)*

SANDY. Just exactly—and of the mines.

MIKE. Reorganized the entire works?

SANDY. He did.

MIKE. National hero, new model: makes drooping family incomes to revive again. Anthracite, sweet anthracite.—How did your sister happen to meet him?

SANDY. She and I went up a month ago to look things over.

MIKE. I see. And was it instant?

SANDY. Immediate.

MIKE. Good for her.—He must be quite a guy.—Which side of this—er—fine, aboriginal family does she resemble most, would you say?

SANDY. *(Looks at him; rises)* The histories of both are in the library; I'll get them out for you. I'll also see if I can round up some of the Living Members. *(Goes up to door Right 2.)*

LIZ. They don't know about *us*, do they? *(Goes above table.)*

SANDY. *(In the doorway stops and turns)* —Pleasanter not, don't you think?

LIZ. Much.

SANDY. That's what *I* thought—also what Kidd thought. *(Moves a step up.)*

MIKE. *(Rising and going near Center)* Look here, Lord—

SANDY. *(Stops)* Yes—?

MIKE. *(Crossing up Center)* Why don't you throw us out?

SANDY. I hope you'll never know. *(A smile and goes out Right 2.)*

LIZ. Meaning what? *(Back of table Left.)*

MIKE. Search me.

LIZ. Maybe Der Kidder has been up to his little tricks. *(Goes up Left.)*

MIKE. *(At mantel)* If only I could get away from his damned paper—

LIZ. It's Sidney himself you can't get away from, dear. *(Up at piano.)*

MIKE. I tried to resign again on the phone this morning.

LIZ. *(Touring up Left at piano)* —Knicknacks—gimcracks—signed photographs! Wouldn't you know you'd have to be rich as the Lords to live in a dump like this? *(Goes to Center. Sees the portrait over the mantel)* Save me—it's a Gilbert Stuart.

MIKE. A what?

LIZ. Catch me, Mike!

MIKE. Faint to the left, will you? *(Crosses down Right to sofa. He returns to the typewritten cards)* "First husband, C. K.—" Can you imagine what a guy named "C. K. Dexter Haven" must be like?

LIZ. "Macaulay Connor" is not such a homespun tag, my pet. *(Goes up Right.)*

MIKE. *(Sits on sofa)* I've been called Mike since I can remember.

LIZ. Well, maybe Dexter is "Ducky" to his friends. *(Goes over Right by steps.)*

MIKE. I wouldn't doubt it.—But I wonder what the "C. K." is for—

LIZ. *(Turns upstage—looks at cabinet)* Maybe it's Pennsylvania Dutch for "William Penn."

MIKE. "C. K. Dexter Haven." God!

LIZ. *(Crossing down to upper corner of sofa)* I knew a plain Joe Smith once. He was only a clerk in a hardware store, but he was an absolute louse.

MIKE. —Also he plays polo. Also designs and races sailboats. "Class" boats, I think they call them. Very upper class, of course.

LIZ. Don't despair. He's out, and Kittredge, man of the people, is in. *(Goes up to mantel.)*

MIKE. From all reports, quite a comer too. Political timber.—Poor fellow, I wonder how he fell for it.

LIZ. I imagine she's a young lady who knows what she wants when she wants it. *(Goes up by piano.)*

MIKE. The young, rich, rapacious American female—there's no other country where she exists.

LIZ.. *(Comes in Center)* I'll admit the idea of *her* scares even me.—Would I change places with her, for all her wealth and beauty? Boy! Just ask me. *(Goes up to piano.)*

MIKE. I know how I'm going to begin. *(Leans*

back on the sofa, closes his eyes, and declaims: LIZ
goes in Center slowly) "—So much for Historical
Philadelphia, so much for Industrial. Now, Gentle
Reader, consider an entire section of American So-
ciety which, closely following the English tradition,
lives on the land, but in a new sense. It is not the
land that provides the living, it is—"

LIZ. *(Back of sofa; pats his arm, then crosses
Right)* You're ahead of yourself. Wait till you do
your documentation.

MIKE. I'm tired. *(Reclines on sofa, head on upstage end)* Kidd is a slave-driver. I wish I was home
in bed. Also I'm hungry. Tell four footmen to call
me in time for lunch.

(LIZ is taking pictures of room off Right 1.)

DINAH. *(Re-enters Left from porch window, the
woman of the world. Crossing Center on her toes—
hand extended)* Oh—how do you do?—Friends of
Alexander's, are you not?

MIKE. *(Rises)* How do you do?—Why, yes, we—

DINAH. *(Crossing Right)* I am Dinah Lord. My
real name is Diana, but my sister changed it.

LIZ. I'm Elizabeth Imbrie—and this is Macaulay
Connor. It's awfully nice of—

DINAH. *(Goes Right to them—extends an arched
hand to each)* Enchantée de vous voir. *(Shakes hands
with* MIKE*)* Enchantée te faire votre connaisance.
(Shakes hands with LIZ*)* —I spoke French before I
spoke English. My early childhood was spent in
Paris, where my father worked in a bank—the
House of Morgan.

LIZ. Really?

DINAH. *C'est vrai—absolument! (Runs up to
piano—jumping over stool Center as she goes)* Can
you play the piano? I can. And sing at the same

time. Listen— *(Plays and sings)* "Pepper Sauce Woman; Pepper Sauce Woman—"

(This dialog goes through the song, topping it:)

LIZ. *(Speaks lowly to* MIKE *Down Right)* What is this?

MIKE. An idiot, probably. They happen in the best of famies, especially in the best.

DINAH. —"Oh, what a shame; she has lost her name. Don't know who to blame, walkin' along to Shango Batcheloor." *(*DINAH *stops singing and continues in a dreamy voice)* The Bahamas—how well I remember them.—Those perfumed nights— the flowers—the native wines. I was there, once, on a little trip with Leopold Stowkowski.

TRACY. *(Enters Left 1; stops up at piano. She has changed into a rather demure dress, high in neck and ample in skirt)* You were there with your governess, after the whooping cough.

*(*DINAH *gestures airily.* LIZ *goes front of sofa.*
MIKE *gets to downstage end.)*

DINAH. *(Crossing to* TRACY *and below her to chair Left of table Left)* —My sister Tracy. Greetings, Sister.

TRACY. Mother wants to see you at once. At once!

DINAH. You've got on my hair ribbon.

TRACY. Your face is still dirty. *(*DINAH *exits Left 1.* TRACY, *cool, collected and charming, all sweetness and light—crossing down to upper corner of sofa)* It's awfully nice having you here. *(Shakes hands with* LIZ *and* MIKE*)* I do hope you'll stay for my wedding.

LIZ. We'd like to very much.

MIKE. In fact, that was our idea.

TRACY. I'm so pleased that it occurred to you.

(Waves them to sit—ALL do so together. She in armchair Right Center. LIZ and MIKE in sofa, together) The house is in rather a mess, of course. We all have to huddle here, and overflow onto the porch. —I hope your rooms are comfortable.

(MIKE takes out pack of cigarettes.)

LIZ. Oh, very, thanks.

TRACY. Anything you want, ask Mary or Elsie. *(Passes cigarette box)* They're magic. What a cunning little camera.

(MIKE has struck match—sees TRACY still holds lighter toward him as she talks to LIZ—he slowly bends forward to accept light for cigarette—then blows his match out—she graciously smiles at him.)

LIZ. *(Lights cigarette from TRACY's lighter)* It's a Contax. I'm afraid I'm rather a nuisance with it.

TRACY. But you couldn't be: I hope you'll take loads. Dear Papá and Mamá aren't allowing any reporters in—that is, except for little Mr. Grace, who does the social news. *(To MIKE)* Can you imagine a grown-up man having to sink so low?

MIKE. It does seem pretty bad.

TRACY. People have always been so kind about letting us live our simple and uneventful little life here unmolested. Of course, after my divorce last year—but I expect that always happens, and is more or less deserved. Dear Papá was quite angry, though, and swore he'd never let another reporter inside the gate. He thought some of their methods were a trifle underhanded.—You're a writer, aren't you, Mr. Connor?

MIKE. *(Looks at her)* In a manner of speaking.

TRACY. Sandy told me. I've sent for your books.

"Macaulay Connor"— What's the "Macaulay" for?

MIKE. My father taught English History. I'm "Mike" to my friends.

TRACY. —Of whom you have many, I'm sure. English history has always fascinated me. Cromwell —Bloody Mary, John the Bastard— Where did he teach? I mean your father—

MIKE. In the high school in South Bend, Indiana.

TRACY. "South Bend"! It sounds like dancing, doesn't it? You must have had a most happy childhood there.

MIKE. It was terrific.

TRACY. I'm so glad.

MIKE. I don't mean it that way.

TRACY. I'm so sorry. Why?

MIKE. Largely due to the lack of the wherewithal, I guess.

TRACY. But that doesn't always cause unhappiness, does it?—not if you're the right kind of man. George Kittredge, my fiancé, never had anything either, but he— Are either of you married?

MIKE. No.

LIZ. I—er—that is, no.

TRACY. You mean *you* were, but now you're divorced?

LIZ. Well, the fact is—

TRACY. Suds—you can't mean you're ashamed of it!

LIZ. Of course I'm not ashamed of it.

MIKE. *(Is staring at her)* Wha-at?

LIZ. It was ages ago, when I was a mere kid, in Duluth. *(Flicks ashes in ash tray.)*

MIKE. Good Lord, Liz—you never told me you were—

LIZ. You never asked.

MIKE. I know, but—

LIZ. Joe Smith, Hardware.

MIKE. Liz, you're the damndest girl. *(Rises.)*

LIZ. *I* think I'm sweet. *(Smiles at* TRACY.*)*

(MIKE *goes to lower end corner of sofa.*)

TRACY. Duluth—that must be a lovely spot. It's west of here, isn't it?

LIZ. Sort of.—But occasionally we get the breezes.

TRACY. Is this your first visit in Philadelphia?

LIZ. Just about.

TRACY. It's a quaint old place, don't you think? I suppose it's affected somewhat by being the only really big city that's near New York.

LIZ. I think that's a very good point to make about it.

TRACY. —Though I suppose you consider us somewhat provincial?

LIZ. Not at all, I assure you.

TRACY. Odd customs, and such. Where the scrapples eat biddle on Sunday. Of course it *is* very old—Philadelphia, I mean, the scrapple is fresh weekly. How old are *you*, Mr. Connor?

MIKE. *(Starts for seat—ashes to tray)* I was thirty last month. *(Sits on sofa again.)*

TRACY. Two books isn't much for a man of thirty. I don't mean to criticize. You probably have other interests outside your work.

MIKE. None.—Unless— *(Looks at* LIZ *and smiles.)*

TRACY. How sweet! Are you living together?

MIKE. *(Through the laugh)* Why—er—no, we're not—

LIZ. That's an odd question, I must say!

TRACY. Why?

LIZ. Well—it just is.

TRACY. I don't see why. I think it's very interesting. *(Leans forward seriously, elbow on knee and chin on hand)* Miss Imbrie—don't you agree that all this marrying and giving in marriage is the damndest gyp that's ever been put over on an unsuspecting public?

MIKE. *(To* LIZ*)* Can she be human!

TRACY. Please, Mr. Connor!—I asked Miss Imbrie a question.

LIZ. No. As a matter of fact, I don't.

TRACY. Good. Nor do I. That's why I'm putting my chin out for the second time tomorrow. (GEORGE, *off Left, calls "Tracy." She rises)* Here's the lucky man now. I'll bring him right in and put him on view—a one-man exhibition. *(As she moves over Left and goes off Left)* In here, George!—In here, my dear!

LIZ. *(To* MIKE*—rises)* My God—who's doing the interviewing here? *(Puts out cigarette on table.)*

MIKE. *(Rises. Back of sofa to Center)* She's a lot more than I counted on.

LIZ. Do you suppose she caught on somehow?

MIKE. No. She's just a hellion. *(Has got to Center.)*

LIZ. I'm beginning to feel the size of a pinhead. *(Goes Right Center.)*

MIKE. Don't let her throw you.

LIZ. Do you want to take over?

MIKE. I want to go home.

(TRACY *re-enters with* GEORGE KITTREDGE, *aged thirty-two; brings him to Center.)*

TRACY. *(As she crosses)* Miss Imbrie—Mr. Connor—Mr. Kittredge, my beau.—Friends of Sandy's, George.

GEORGE. *(Center)* Any friend of Sandy's— *(Shakes hands with them.)*

LIZ. *(Right Center)* How do you do?

MIKE. *(Center)* How are you?

GEORGE. Fine as silk, thanks.

LIZ. You certainly look it.

GEORGE. Thanks, I've shaken quite a lot of coal-dust from my feet in the last day or two.

TRACY. *(Left Center)* Isn't he beautiful? Isn't it wonderful what a little soap and water will do?

MIKE. Didn't I read a piece about you in *The Nation* a while ago?

GEORGE. Quite a while ago: I've been resting on my laurels since that—and a couple of others.

MIKE. Quite a neat piece of work—anticipating the Guffey Coal Act the way you did.—Or do I remember straight?

GEORGE. Anyone should have foreseen that—I was just lucky.

LIZ. A becoming modesty.

GEORGE. That's nothing to what's yet to be done with Labor relations.

TRACY. You ought to see him with the men—they simply adore him.

GEORGE. Oh—come on, Tracy!

TRACY. *(Backing a few steps to Left)* Oh, but they do! Never in my life will I forget that first night I saw you, all those wonderful faces, and the torchlights, and the way his voice boomed—

GEORGE. You see, I'm really a spellbinder.—That's the way I got her.

TRACY. *(Crossing up to GEORGE)* Except it was me who got you!—I'm going to put these two at the bridal table, in place of the Grants.

GEORGE. That's a good idea.

TRACY. *(Crossing to Left, back of table)* George, it won't rain, will it?—Promise me it won't rain. *(Looking out window.)*

GEORGE. *(Follows her)* Tracy, I'll see to that personally.

TRACY. I almost believe you could.

MIKE. I guess this must be love.

GEORGE. Your guess is correct, Mr. Connor.
TRACY. I'm just his faithful Old Dog Tray.
GEORGE. Give me your paw?
TRACY. *(She does)* You've got it.

(GEORGE *takes her hand and kisses it.*)

(MARGARET *enters Right 1, followed by* DINAH.
DINAH *remains in doorway.* MARGARET *goes
directly to between* LIZ *and* MIKE *in front of
sofa, Right.*)

MARGARET. *(Shakes hands with* BOTH*)* How do
you do? We're so happy to have you. Forgive me
for not coming in sooner, but things are in such a
state. I'd no idea that a simple country wedding
could involve so much. *(Crosses to* TRACY *and*
TRACY *comes to her. They meet Center and beam)*
My little girl— (SANDY *enters Right 2 and crosses
down to table Left near* TRACY. GEORGE *works to
Left of table Left)* —I do hope you'll be comfor-
able. Those rooms are inclined to be hot in this
weather.—Aren't you pretty, my dear! Look at the
way she wears her hair, Tracy. Isn't it pretty?
TRACY. Mighty fine.
MARGARET. I do wish my husband might be here
to greet you, but we expect him presently. He's been
detained in New York on business for that lovely
Tina Mara. You know her work?
LIZ. Only vaguely!
MARGARET. So talented—and such a lovely person! But like so many artists—no business head,
none whatever. *(Gives* TRACY *a knowing smile.*
TRACY *and* SANDY *smile.* SANDY *then smirks.* ED-
WARD *enters from Right 2. He carries tray with
sherry decanter and eight glasses.* THOMAS *follows
to serve. They go up Center)* Good morning, George!
GEORGE. Good morning, Mrs. Lord!

MARGARET. And this is my youngest daughter, Diana—

(DINAH *curtseys.*)

MIKE. *(Is working his way behind sofa to down Right)* I think we've met.

(THOMAS *gives* MARGARET *drink and napkin.*)

MARGARET. Thank you, Thomas.

(DINAH *then works her way across back of sofa to armchair Left Center—stops to get glass of sherry for* SANDY.*)*

SANDY. *(Sitting in armchair Left Center)* Now let's all relax, and throw ourselves into things. Hi, George!

(MARGARET *sits in armchair Right Center.* TRACY *sits stool Center.* GEORGE *works slowly to behind her.*)

GEORGE. Hello, Sandy— Welcome home!

(THOMAS *serves* LIZ. DINAH *serves* SANDY *with sherry.*)

MARGARET. After lunch Sandy must show you some of the sights—the model dairy, and the stables, and the chicken farm—and perhaps there'll be time to run you out to some other places on the Main Line—Devins, Saint Davids. Bryn Mawr, where my daughter Tracy went to college—

(THOMAS *serves* MIKE, *then* THOMAS *goes up for* WILLIE'S *wine.*)

DINAH. 'Til she got bounced out on her—

MARGARET. —Dinah!

UNCLE WILLIE. *(Entering Right)* It's a pretty kettle of fish when a man has to wait two mortal hours—

TRACY. *(Rising)* Papá!—Dear Papá—

UNCLE WILLIE. What's that?

TRACY. *(As she rushes over Right to embrace him)* Didn't the car meet you?

WILLIE. *(Amazed, but hardly audible)* The car?

TRACY. *(Crossing down Right)* You angel—to drop everything and get here in time for lunch— Isn't he, Mamá?

MARGARET. In—indeed he is.

UNCLE WILLIE. I'm not one to jump to conclusions, but—

TRACY. These are our friends, Mr. Connor and Miss Imbrie, Father.—They're here for the wedding.

MIKE. How are you, Mr. Lord?

LIZ. How do you do, Mr. Lord?

UNCLE WILLIE. Dashed fine. How are you? *(Shakes hands with MIKE.)*

SANDY. *(Over Left)* Hi, Pops!

UNCLE WILLIE. *(Crossing in Center)* —Alexander.

DINAH. *(Crossing in Center)* Welcome back, Daddy!

UNCLE WILLIE. Dinah— Kittredge— *(He turns to MARGARET and bows)* Margaret, my sweet.

(THOMAS *comes down to his Left with a sherry. UNCLE WILLIE takes sherry and tosses it off: glass back to* THOMAS, *who, taking stool from Center, goes up to fireplace.)*

TRACY. Mother, don't you think you ought to explain the new arrangement to Father before lunch?

MARGARET. *(Taking* WILLIE *by the arm)* Why—yes—I think I'd best. *(Having* WILLIE *by arm, takes him over Left as* DEXTER *enters. They meet Left 1)* See here—here is the list now—Seth.

(TRACY *goes up Center.)*

SANDY. *(As he sees* DEXTER *enter)* Holy cats!
MARGARET. *(As she sees him enter she turns quickly to look at* TRACY, *then speaks)* Dexter Haven!
DEXTER. *(Down at Left 1 entrance)* Hello, friends and enemies. I came the short way, across the fields.
MARGARET. Well, this *is* a surprise.
GEORGE. *(Up Center)* I should think it is.
DEXTER. Hello, you sweet thing. *(Taking* MARGARET *by the shoulders and kissing her cheek.)*

(MIKE *and* LIZ *cross.)*

MARGARET. Now you go right home at once!
UNCLE WILLIE. Remove yourself, young man!
DEXTER. But I've been invited. *(Going to* WILLIE *and shaking hands)* How are you, sir?
UNCLE WILLIE. No better, no worse. Get along.
DEXTER. Hello, Sandy.
SANDY. *(Shaking hands with* DEXTER*)* How are you, boy?
DEXTER. Never better. In fact, it's immoral how good I feel.
DINAH. *(Works down Center)* What—what brings you here, Mr. Haven?
DEXTER. *(Crossing to her Center)* Dinah, my angel! *(Kisses her cheek)* Why, she's turned into a raving beauty! *(Crossing to* TRACY *as* DINAH *goes up Center)* Awfully sweet and thoughtful of you to ask me to lunch, Tray.

TRACY. Not at all.—Extra place, Thomas.

(GEORGE *crosses down Center.*)

THOMAS. Yes, Miss Tracy. *(He and* EDWARD *go out Right 2.)*

TRACY. *(Right Center)* Miss Imbrie—Mr. Connor—my former husband, whose name for the moment escapes me.

DEXTER. *(Center)* How do you do?

MIKE. *(Right)* How do you do?

LIZ. *(Right Center)* How do you do? *(Together)*

DEXTER. —Of course I intended to come anyway, but it did make it pleasanter.—Hello, Kittredge. *(Turns Center.)*

GEORGE. How are you, Haven?

DEXTER. *(Peers at him)* What's the matter? You don't look as well as when I last saw you. *(He pats his arm sympathetically)* Poor fellow—I know just how you feel. *(He turns to* TRACY; *gazes at her fondly)* Redhead—isn't *she* in the pink, though!— *You* don't look old enough to marry anyone, even for the first time—you never did! She needs trouble to mature her, Kittredge. Give her lots of it.

GEORGE. I'm afraid she can't count on me for that.

DEXTER. No? Too bad.—Sometimes, for your own sake, I think you should have stuck to me longer, Red.

TRACY. I thought it was for life. *(Crossing to* GEORGE—*Left of him—takes his arm)* but the nice Judge gave me a full pardon.

DEXTER. That's the kind of talk I like to hear; no bitterness, no recrimination—just a good quick left to the jaw.

GEORGE. Very funny.

THOMAS. *(Appears in the door Right 2)* Luncheon is served, Madam.

MARGARET. Thank you, Thomas.

UNCLE WILLIE. *(Crossing to Center)* I don't suppose a man ever had a better or finer family. *(Turns and takes MARGARET'S arm)* I wake in the night and say to myself—"Seth, you lucky dog. What have you done to deserve it?" *(Goes up and exits Right 2, taking MARGARET along.)*

MARGARET. *(As they go)* And what *have* you? *(Exits.)*

(WARN Curtain.)

TRACY. *(Crossing to Right)* Do you mind if I go in with Mr. Connor, Miss Imbrie?

LIZ. Why, not in the least.

SANDY. *(Crossing and goes up Right back of couch, takes LIZ's arm. BOTH exit)* Sandy's your boy.

TRACY. *(Taking MIKE's arm and up Center)* —Because I think he's such an interesting man.

GEORGE. Come on, Dinah, I draw you, I guess.

DINAH. *(Taking DEXTER's arm also)* Dexter—

DEXTER. *(As they go)* Isn't snatching one of my girls enough, you cad?

GEORGE. *(At the same cue and time as they go up Right)* You're a very bright fellow, Haven, I'll hire you. *(He exits.)*

TRACY. *(To MIKE—going up)* That's very insulting—but consistently interesting. We **must talk** more.

MIKE. *(Going up)* No wonder you want to get away from all this.

(They are ALL up near door Right 2 when SETH comes into room from Left 1.)

SETH. *(Stopping MIKE, DEXTER, DINAH, TRACY.*

OTHERS *have gone)* I don't know how welcome I am, but after Sandy's note, I thought the least I could do was to—

(DINAH starts down but is stopped by TRACY.)

TRACY. *(As she restrains DINAH) Uncle Willie:*
(She turns to OTHERS) Please go on in, everyone, I want a word with Uncle Willie.

(They go in—DEXTER turning back with a faint smile at TRACY. She crosses down Left, facing SETH.)

SETH. Well, daughter?
TRACY. Well?
SETH. Still Justice, with her shining sword—eh? Who's on the spot?
TRACY. We are; thanks to you—Uncle Willie.

QUICK CURTAIN

ACT TWO

SCENE I

*The porch, which is more like a room than a porch.
Entrance from the sitting room at back Right
Center and Left Center to the library, through
glass doors at stage Left; to garden, down broad
stone steps from porch and along gravel path
past shrubbery to Left and Right. Open side of
porch shielded. At Right is a step down to
path; a door (Right) at upper end of this path;
a sofa against extreme Right wall. Flower
stands Right and Left on porch; a stool Right;
table and chairs Center; chaise longue Left. Pots
of geraniums, large and small.*

Early evening, Friday. The sky has cleared.

AT RISE: MIKE *is in Left Center chair on porch,
making additional notes.* LIZ *is seated on steps
over Right, reloading her camera.*

LIZ. I may need more film.

MIKE. I may need more paper.

LIZ. There's a cousin Joanna, who's definitely
crazy.

MIKE. Who told you?

LIZ. Dinah.

MIKE. Dinah should know.

LIZ. Where is she now? I want some more shots
of her, while it's still light.

46

MIKE. She's out schooling a horse somewhere. It's the horses that get the schooling hereabouts. Did you shoot the old Tycoon milking his cows?

LIZ. Several times. He shot one at me, but he missed.

MIKE. Caption: "Seventy Times Seven Fat Kine Has He." *(Consults his notes)* "George Kittredge, Important Official, Important Company. Controlling interest owned by Seth Lord."

LIZ. What a coincidence and will wonders never cease?

MIKE. I'm inclined to like Kittredge—I can see how she fell for him. I think he's in a tough spot, with Haven prowling around, though.

LIZ. Is a sinister fellow, Dexter.

MIKE. Is very.—But George is interesting. Get him on coal some time.

LIZ. I'd rather have him on toast.

MIKE. *(Rises, crossing Center)* Answer me honestly, Liz; what right has a girl like Tracy Lord to exist?

LIZ. Politically, socially, or economically?

MIKE. *(Crossing in Right to LIZ)* But what place has she got in the world today? Come the Revolution she'll be the first to go.

LIZ. Sure; right out under the Red General's arm.

MIKE. She's a new one on me. *(Crossing to Left of table Left)* Maybe Philadelphia produces a different brand of monkey.

LIZ. *(Looks at him keenly)* You're a funny one, Mike.

MIKE. Why?

LIZ. Use the name "Wanamaker" in a sentence.

MIKE. I bite.

LIZ. I met a girl this morning. I hate her, but I—

MIKE. I get you, but you're wrong. You couldn't be wronger. *(Crossing Left of table)* Women like that bore the pants off me.

LIZ. For a writer, you use your figures of speech most ineptly. You know, I wish they knew why we were here. They're all such sweet innocents, it makes me feel like—

(WILLIE, *with a red rose, and* SETH *enter from the garden down Right.* LIZ *rises.*)

UNCLE WILLIE. Would you accept this perfect rose, Miss Imbrie?

(MIKE *crosses and sits on chaise down Left.*)

LIZ. Why, thank you, Mr. Lord. It's a beauty. *(Takes it.)*
SETH. Miss Imbrie is amused at something.
LIZ. I'm sorry, Mr. Tracy, but it's so funny, you being uncle and nephew. Could I have a picture of you together? (*Leaves rose on porch.*)
UNCLE WILLIE. Certainly! *(Slips his arm through* SETH's*)* Now stand up straight, Willie. He *is* younger than I. It was a matter of half sisters marrying step-brothers.
LIZ. *(Front of them, near Center)* I see. That is, I think I do. *(Snaps a picture.)*
UNCLE WILLIE. No incest, however.
LIZ. Of course not. *(Snaps another.)*
UNCLE WILLIE. There have been other things, however. *(Looks at* SETH*)* Uncle Willie—I'm thinking of asking that little dancer, Tina Mara, to come down and dance for the wedding guests tomorrow. Do you think it's a good idea?
SETH. Excellent. It might put an end to the ridiculous gossip about you and her. *(Looks between them.)*
UNCLE WILLIE. Is there gossip?
SETH. There seems to be.
UNCLE WILLIE. Is it ridiculous?

(SANDY comes from the library Left and crosses to above table.)

SETH. All gossip is ridiculous.

SANDY. Look alive, men! Time to dress!

SETH. Right you are. Thanks, Sandy— *(Goes up into the house Right Center window to Right.)*

(SANDY follows. LIZ picks up rose.)

UNCLE WILLIE. Miss Imbrie, as a camera-fiend, I think I have another interesting subject for you.

LIZ. Will I have time?

UNCLE WILLIE. Time is an illusion. Come with me, please. *(She takes his arm)* It's part of the old house, a little removed from it.

LIZ. But what?

UNCLE WILLIE. An ancient granite privy, of superb design—a dream of loveliness.

LIZ. —At sunset—idyllic!

(LIZ follows UNCLE WILLIE out Right 1. MIKE crosses and picks up cards on Center table as he leaves table, going up Right. TRACY enters Left.)

TRACY. *(Crossing to back of Center table)* Please wait a minute.

MIKE. *(Back Right of Center table)* With pleasure. *(Turns where he is. She goes to him; looks at him wonderingly)* What's the matter?

TRACY. I've been reading these stories. They're so damned beautiful.

MIKE. You like? Thanks—

TRACY. Why, Connor, they're almost poetry.

MIKE. *(Laughs shortly)* Don't fool yourself; they are! *(Goes down Right below chair.)*

TRACY. I can't make you out at all, now.

MIKE. Really? I thought I was easy.

TRACY. So did I, but you're not. *(Crossing down Center)* You talk so big and tough—and then you write like this. Which is which?

MIKE. I guess I'm both.

TRACY. No—I believe you put the toughness on, to save your skin.

MIKE. You think?

TRACY. Yes. *I* know a little about that—

MIKE. Do you?

TRACY. Quite a lot. *(They look at each other for a moment. Then* TRACY *laughs a little embarrassedly and glances away)* It—the book—it was just such a complete—hell of a surprise, that's all. *(Goes down Left.)*

MIKE. Yes—it seems you do. *(Sits Right of table.)*

TRACY. *(Turns to him)* What?

MIKE. Know about it.

TRACY. *(Down Left Center)* The one called "With the Rich and Mighty"—I think I liked *it* best.

MIKE. I got that from a Spanish peasant's proverb—"With the Rich and Mighty always a little Patience."

TRACY. *(Crossing into Center, sits Left of table)* Good! Tell me something, will you? When you can do a thing like this how can you possibly do anything else? *(Leaves book on table.)*

MIKE. Such as what?

TRACY. You said after lunch—what was it you said?—"Cheap stuff for expensive magazines."

MIKE. Did I?

TRACY. Yes. You did. You said you spent most of your time that way.

MIKE. Practically all. Why? What about it?

TRACY. I can't understand it. And I like to understand things.

MIKE. You'll never believe it, but there are people in this world who have to earn their living.

TRACY. Of course! But people buy books, don't they?

MIKE. Sure they do! They even read them.

TRACY. Well, then?

MIKE. That one represents two solid years' work. It netted Connor something under six hundred dollars.

TRACY. But that shouldn't *be!*

MIKE. —Only unhappily it is.

(There is a pause.)

TRACY. And what about your Miss Imbrie?

MIKE. Miss Imbrie is in somewhat the same fix. She is a born painter, and might be an important one. But Miss Imbrie must eat. Also, she prefers a roof over her head to being constantly out in the rain and snow.

TRACY. *(Rising and going down Left a little, then up behind her chair)* Food and a roof—food and a roof—

MIKE. Those charming essentials.

TRACY. *(Turns to him)* Listen: I've got an idea! *(Crosses to him Center; over the table)* Listen: I've got the most marvelous little house in Unionville. It's up on a hill, with a view that would knock you silly. I'm never there except in the hunting season, and not much then, and I'd be so happy to know it was of some use to someone. *(Crosses Right, then turns back)* There's a brook and a small lake, no size really, and a patch of woods, and in any kind of weather, it's the— *(Goes down Center step, looking out front at the sky)* —And look at that sky now, will you! Suddenly it's clear as clear! It's going to be fine tomorrow! It's going to be fair! Good for you, God! *(Glances down Left 1 and sees someone coming)* Hell! *(Goes back up onto the porch)* Someone's coming—someone I don't want to be alone with. Stand by for a couple of minutes. Will you?

MIKE. *(Rising)* Certainly—if you like.

TRACY. *(Right Center)* You *will* think about the house, won't you?

MIKE. Why, it's terribly nice of you, but—

TRACY. Don't think I'd come trouping in every minute because I wouldn't. I'd never come, except when expressly asked to.

MIKE. It isn't that. *(Crosses to Left Center.)*

TRACY. *(Follows a step)* What is it?

MIKE. Well, you see—er—you see the idea of artists having a patron has more or less gone out, and—

TRACY. *(Looks at him, hurt)* I see. *(Pauses a moment)* That wasn't especially kind of you, Mr. Connor. There's no need to rub our general uselessness in.

MIKE. I'm afraid I don't get you.

TRACY. Don't bother. I'm sorry to have seemed—patronizing.

MIKE. I didn't quite mean—

TRACY. Please don't bother, really.

(MIKE *goes up Left.*)

DEXTER. *(Enters from Left 1; carries a small tissue-wrapped picture)* Hello.

TRACY. Hello, fancy seeing you here. *(She crosses over Right.)*

DEXTER. *(Mounts the porch to table Center)* Orange juice? Certainly! *(Pours and drinks.)*

TRACY. You're sure you don't want something stronger? I'll ring if you like. *(Sits on stool Right.)*

DEXTER. Not now, thanks. This is fine. *(Front of Center table.)*

TRACY. Don't tell me you've forsaken your beloved whiskey-and-whiskies—

DEXTER. No, indeed. I've just changed their color, that's all. I go in for the pale pastel shades now. I find they're more becoming. (DEXTER *drinks, facing upstage; sees* MIKE) We met at lunch, didn't we?

MIKE. *(Crossing down back of chair Left Center)* Yes, I seem to remember. Connor's my name.

DEXTER. —The writer—of course! Do you drink, Mr. Connor?

MIKE. A little. Why?

DEXTER. Not to excess?

MIKE. Not often.

DEXTER. —And a writer! It's extraordinary. I thought all writers drank to excess, and beat their wives. I expect that at one time I secretly wanted to be a writer. *(He looks up at him and grins. Glances at* TRACY, *drinks, then puts glass on table.)*

TRACY. Dexter, would you mind doing something for me?

DEXTER. Anything, what? *(Puts picture on table Center; goes down Right Center.)*

TRACY. Get the hell out of here.

DEXTER. Oh, no, I couldn't do that. That wouldn't be fair to you. You need me too much.

TRACY. *(Seated on stool)* Would you mind telling me just what it is you're hanging around for? (MIKE *moves toward Left)* No—please don't go! I'd honestly much prefer it if you wouldn't.

(MIKE *sits on chaise Left.)*

DEXTER. *(Crossing to Center below table)* So should I. Do stay, Mr. Connor. As a writer this ought to be right up your street. *(Turns to* TRACY.*)*

TRACY. Don't miss a word!

DEXTER. Honestly, you never looked better in your life; you're getting a fine tawny look—

TRACY. *(Rises, crossing to Right of table Center)* Oh, we're going to talk about me, are we? Goody.

DEXTER. *(Right)* —It's astonishing what money can do for people, don't you agree, Mr. Connor? Not too much, you know,—just more than enough. Particularly for girls. Look at Tracy. There's never been a blow that hasn't been softened for her. There'll never be one that won't be softened—why, it even changed her shape—she was a dumpy little thing originally.

TRACY. —Only as it happens, I'm not interested in myself, for the moment. What interests me now is what, if any, your real point is, in—

DEXTER. Not interested in yourself! My dear, you're fascinated! You're far and away your favorite person in the world.

TRACY. Dexter, in case you don't know it—I—!

DEXTER. *(Crossing in Center)* Shall I go on—?

TRACY. Oh, yes, please do, by all means— *(Sits Right of table.)*

DEXTER. Of course, she is kindness itself, Mr. Connor— *(Goes Left.)*

TRACY. —Itself, Mr. Connor.

DEXTER. *(Left)* She is generous to a fault—that is, except to other people's faults. For instance, she never had the slightest sympathy toward nor understanding of what used to be known as my deep and gorgeous thirst.

TRACY. That was your problem!

DEXTER. *(Turns, crossing into Center, above table)* It was the problem of a young man in exceptionally high spirits, who drank to slow down that damned engine he'd found nothing yet to do with—I refer to my mind. You took on that problem with me, when you took me— You were no helpmate there, Tracy— you were a scold.

TRACY. It was disgusting. It made you so unattractive.

DEXTER. A weakness—sure. And strength is her

religion, Mr. Connor. She is a goddess, without patience for any kind of human imperfection. And when I gradually discovered that my relation to her was expected to be not that of a loving husband and a good companion, but— *(Turns away from her to Left, muttering)* Oh—never mind—

TRACY. Say it!

DEXTER. *(Turns to her)* —But that of a kind of high priest to a virgin goddess, then my drinks grew more frequent and deeper in hue, that's all.

TRACY. *(Rises, crossing down Right a bit)* I never considered you as that, nor myself!

DEXTER. You did without knowing it. *(Crossing to her over Right)* And the night that *you* got drunk on champagne, and climbed out on the roof and stood there naked, with your arms out to the moon, wailing like a banshee—

(MIKE slides off the chaise and into the room Left.)

TRACY. I told you I never had the slightest recollection of doing any such thing!

DEXTER. I know; you drew a blank. You wanted to— Mr. Connor, what would you say in the case of— *(Turns and sees MIKE gone. Crosses to Left of table Center.)*

TRACY. He's a reporter, incidentally. He's doing us for *Destiny.*

DEXTER. *(Sits Left of table)* Sandy told me. A pity we can't supply photographs of you on the roof.

TRACY. *(Crossing to front of table)* Honestly, the fuss you made over that silly, childish—

DEXTER. It was enormously important, and most revealing. The moon is also a goddess, chaste and virginal.

TRACY. Stop using those foul words! We were married nearly a year, weren't we?

DEXTER. Marriage doesn't change a true case like

yours, my dear. It's an affair of the spirit—not of the flesh.

TRACY. Dexter, what are you trying to make me out as?

DEXTER. Tracy, what do you fancy yourself as?

TRACY. *(Crossing below table to Left at chaise)* I don't know that I fancy myself as anything.

DEXTER. *(Rises, crossing Left to her)* When I read you were going to marry Kittredge, I couldn't believe it. How in the world can you even think of it?

TRACY. *(Turns on him)* I love him, that's why! As I never even began to love you. *(Sits on chaise.)*

DEXTER. It may be true, but I doubt it. *I* think it's just a swing from me, and what I represent—but I think it's too violent a swing. That's why I came on. Kittredge is no great tower of strength, you know, Tray. He's just a tower.

TRACY. You've known him how long?—Half a day.

DEXTER. I knew him for two days two years ago, the time I went up to the fields with your father, *(Sits on arm of chair Left of table)* but half a day would've done, I think.

TRACY. It's just personal, then—

DEXTER. Purely and completely.

TRACY. You couldn't possibly understand him or his qualities. I shouldn't expect you to.

DEXTER. I suppose when you come right down to it, Tray, it just offends my vanity to have anyone who was ever remotely my wife, remarry so obviously beneath her.

TRACY. "Beneath" me! How dare you—any of you—in this day and age use such a—?

DEXTER. I'm talking about difference in mind and imagination. You could marry Mac, the nightwatchman, and I'd cheer for you.

TRACY. *(Rises, crossing in Left Center)* **And** what's wrong with George?

DEXTER. *(On arm of Left Center chair)* Nothing —utterly nothing. He's a wizard at his job, and I'm sure he is honest, sober and industrious. He's just not for you.

TRACY. He *is* for me—he's a great man and a good man; already he's of national importance.

DEXTER. Good Lord—you sound like *Destiny* talking. *(Rises)* Well, whatever he is, you'll have to stick, Tray. He'll give you no out as I did.

TRACY. I won't require one. *(Gets Right Center.)*

DEXTER. *(Crossing in front of table Center—leans on it)* I suppose you'd still be attractive to any man of spirit, though. There's something engaging about it, this virgin goddess business, something more challenging to the male than the more obvious charms.

TRACY. Really?

DEXTER. Oh, yes! We're very vain, you know— "This citadel can and shall be taken—and I'm just the boy to do it."

TRACY. *(Over Right)* You seem quite contemptuous of me, all of a sudden.

DEXTER. *(Crossing to her)* Not of you, Red, never of you. You could be the damndest, finest woman on this earth. If I'm contemptuous of anything, it's of something in you you either can't help, or make no attempt to; your so-called "strength"—your prejudice against weakness—your blank intolerance—

TRACY. Is that all?

DEXTER. That's the gist of it; because you'll never be a first class woman or a first class human being, till you have learned to have some regard for human frailty. It's a pity your own foot can't slip a little sometime—but no, your sense of inner divinity won't allow it. The goddess must and shall remain intact.—You know, I think there are more of you around than people realize. You're a special class of American female now—the Married Maidens.—And of Type Philadelphiaensis, you're the absolute tops, my dear.

TRACY. Damn your soul, Dext, if you say another—!

(GEORGE *comes in Left Center from the living room.* *He looks at them and smiles with a great attempt at good humor.*)

DEXTER. I'm through, Tracy—for the moment I've said my say.

GEORGE. *(Crossing in Left Center)* I suppose I ought to object to this twosome.

DEXTER. *(Crossing in Right Center)* That would be most objectionable. Well, anytime either of you want more advice from me—

GEORGE. When we do, we'll give you a ring, Haven.

DEXTER. *(Crossing down Center to Right)* Do that, will you? You'll find that I have a most sympathetic and understanding ear— *(Turns, facing her)* I left you a little wedding present there on the table, Red—I'm sorry I hadn't any ribbon to tie it up with. *(Goes out Right 1.)*

GEORGE. *(Right Center)* You see—it's no use even attempting to be friendly.

TRACY. *(Crossing in Right of table)* Certainly not. You were a dear to try. Please don't mind him.

DINAH. *(Enters Right 1, crossing to Center as she speaks)* You got taken when you bought that roan. She's parrot-jawed.

TRACY. Get into a tub. You're revolting.

DINAH. *(Crossing up Left)* What's more, she swallows wind by the bucket.

TRACY. Where's Miss Imbrie? Wasn't she with you?

DINAH. No. She's gone to the privy with Uncle Willie. *(Goes out Left Center to Left.)*

TRACY. *(Front of table. Picks up the package DEXTER left on table)* It's anyone's guess what this might be. *(Unwraps the package)* It's, why—it's a photograph of the "True Love."

GEORGE. *(Crossing to her)* —The?— What's that?

TRACY. A boat he designed—and built, practically. We sailed her up the coast of Maine and back, the summer we were married. My, she was yare.

GEORGE. "Yare"? What does that mean?

TRACY. It means— Oh, what does it mean?— Easy to handle—quick to the helm—fast—bright— everything a boat should be. *(Gazes at the photograph for a moment without speaking, then drops it upon table)* —And the hell with it. *(Goes up Left.)*

GEORGE. Rather bad taste, I'd say, giving you that.

TRACY. Dexter never concerns himself much with taste.

GEORGE. How'd you ever happen to marry a fellow like that, Tracy?

TRACY. Oh, I don't know—I expect it was kind of a hangover from childhood days. We grew up together, you know.

GEORGE. I see—propinquity.

TRACY. *(Crossing in to him Center)* Oh, George— to get away—to get away—! Somehow to feel useful in the world—

GEORGE. Useful?—I'm going to build you an ivory tower with my own two hands.

TRACY. Like fun you are.

GEORGE. You mean you've been in one too long?

TRACY. I mean that, and a lot of things.

GEORGE. I'm going to make a grand life, dear— and you can help, all right.

TRACY. I hope I can.

GEORGE. From now on we'll both stop wasting time on unimportant people.

TRACY. *(Beside him)* That's all right with me.

GEORGE. Our little house on the river up there. I'd like people to consider it an honor to be asked there.

TRACY. Why an honor, especially?

GEORGE. We're going to represent something, Tracy—something straight and sound and fine.— *(Looks off Right)* And then perhaps young Mr. Haven may be somewhat less condescending.

TRACY. *(Looks at him)* George,—you don't really mind him, do you? I mean the fact of him—

GEORGE. The—? I don't see what you mean, Tray.

TRACY. *(Crossing Left)* I mean that—you know— that he ever was—was my lord and master—that we ever were—

GEORGE. *(Crosses to her)* I don't believe he ever was—not really. I don't believe anyone ever was, or ever will be. That's the wonderful thing about you, Tray.

TRACY. *(Looks at him, startled)* What? How—?

GEORGE. You're like some marvelous, distant— *(She sits on chaise)* Oh, queen, I guess. You're so cool and fine and—and always so much your own. That's the wonderful *you* in you—that no one can ever really possess—that no one can touch, hardly. It's—it's a kind of beautiful purity, Tracy, that's the only word for it.

TRACY. *(Now really frightened)* George—

GEORGE. *(Sits on upstage side of chaise)* Oh, it's grand, Tracy—it's just grand! Everyone feels it about you. It's what I first worshipped you for, Tracy, from afar.

TRACY. George, listen—

GEORGE. First, now, and always! *(Leans toward her)* Only from a little nearer, now—eh, darling?

TRACY. I don't want to be worshipped! I want to be loved!

GEORGE. You're that, too. You're that, all right.

TRACY. I mean really loved.

GEORGE. But that goes without saying, Tracy.

TRACY. And now it's you— (EDWARD, *carrying a tray with drinks, enters Right Center, followed by* ELISE. *They come Center.* ELSIE *picks up orange juice tray from table*) who doesn't see what *I* mean. You can just leave them, Edward. *(Rises.)*

(EDWARD *places tray on Center table.)*

ELSIE. *(Reaching for wrapped picture)* Shall I put this picture with the other presents, Miss Tracy?

TRACY. *(Crossing Center to table)* No—just leave it there, please.

ELSIE. Yes, Miss. *(Exits Right Center.)*

(EDWARD *follows.)*

GEORGE. *(Crossing to Center)* Don't let Miss Imbrie get hold of it.

TRACY. *(Right of table, wrapping picture)* I should say not.

GEORGE. *(Crossing in to her)* I hope they'll soft pedal the first marriage angle.

TRACY. I wish they'd pedal themselves right out of here.

GEORGE. They've got a job to do, and it's an honor, you know, Tracy.

TRACY. What is?

GEORGE. Why—to be done by *Destiny.*

TRACY. Are you joking?

GEORGE. Joking—?

TRACY. But you can't seriously mean that you think—!

GEORGE. I think *Destiny* fills a very definite place, Tracy.

MARGARET. *(Enters Left, with* SETH*)* George, you aren't dressed!—And Tracy, you're the guest of honor—you mustn't be late.

GEORGE. *(Crossing down step and to Left)* Right on my way, Ma'm! Wait for me, Tracy. I make the Gatehouse in nothing flat, now. *(Exits Left 1.)*

SETH. Does he by any chance ever walk anywhere?

TRACY. When he likes, I expect.

(MARGARET *goes Left to chaise and sits.*)

SETH. *(Left Center)* I have a feeling he's going to take the ring tomorrow and go through center with it.

MARGARET. Seth, you idiot.

TRACY. That's very amusing, I'm sure. *(Over to Right Center.)*

SETH. *(Crossing in Center)* Oh, don't take things to heart so, Tracy. You'll wear yourself out.

LIZ. *(Entering Right 1)* I won't be a minute. *(Crosses up to window, Right Center.)*

MARGARET. There's no hurry, Miss Imbrie.

(LIZ *exits Right Center.* TRACY *sits stool Right.*)

SETH. *(Back of Center table, stirring cocktails)* What bothers me at the moment is the spectacle we're all making of ourselves for the benefit of the young man and woman from *Destiny*.

TRACY. Whose fault is it?

SETH. That's beside the point.

MARGARET. Never in my life have I felt so self-conscious. It's all simply dreadful.

SETH. It's worse; it's stupid and childish and completely undignified.

TRACY. So are other things.

SETH. They can publish what they like about me, but—

TRACY. *(Rises. Crossing up Center)* —My idea is, they'll publish nothing about any of us.

SETH. How do you propose to stop them? *(Pours two cocktails.)*

TRACY. I don't quite know yet. *(Sits Right of table.)*

SETH. Well, at present the least we can do is to inform Connor and the camera-lady that we are all quite aware of their purpose here. I insist on that.

TRACY. All right! I'll tell them myself.

SETH. I think it will come better from me, don't you—as, at least, titular head of the family? *(Crosses down Left with drink for MARGARET.)*

TRACY. *(A moment. Then TRACY speaks deliberately, harshly)* Of course—inasmuch as you let us in for it in the first place.

SETH. *(Crossing in Left Center)* Do keep that note out of your voice, Tracy. It's most unattractive.

TRACY. Oh? How does Miss Mara talk? Or does she purr?

MARGARET. Tracy!

SETH. *(Turning to Left)* It's all right, Margaret.

TRACY. Sweet and low, I suppose. Dulcet. Very ladylike. —You've got a fine right, you have—after the way you've treated Mother—after the way you've treated us all—a magnificent right you've got to come back here in your best country manner and strike attitudes and make stands and criticize my fiancé and give orders and mess things up generally, just as if you'd done—

MARGARET. Stop it instantly, Tracy!

TRACY. *(Rises)* I can't help it. It's sickening.—As if he'd done nothing at all!

MARGARET. It is no concern of yours. If it concerns anyone, it concerns—well, actually, I don't know whom it concerns, except your father.

SETH. *(Crossing in Left Center towards MARGARET)* That's very wise of you, Margaret. What most wives won't seem to realize is that their husband's philandering—particularly the middle-aged kind—has nothing whatever to do with them.

TRACY. *(Crossing down a step, Right Center)* Oh? Then what has it to do with?

SETH. *(Crossing in Center and sits Left of table)* A reluctance to grow old, I think. I suppose the best mainstay a man can have as he gets along in years is a daughter—the right kind of daughter.

TRACY. *(Crossing over Right Center)* That's interesting, to say the least.

SETH. —One who loves him blindly—as no good wife ever should, of course.—One for whom he can do no wrong—

TRACY. How sweet.

SETH. I'm talking seriously about something I've thought out thoroughly. I've had to. I think a devoted young daughter gives a man the illusion that youth is still his.

TRACY. Very important, I suppose.

SETH. Very—and without her, he's inclined to go in search of it again, because it's as precious to him as it is to any woman.—But with a girl of his own full of warmth for him, full of foolish, unquestioning, uncritical affection—

TRACY. —None of which I've got.

SETH. None. You have a good mind, a pretty face and a disciplined body that does what you tell it. You have more wealth than any of us, thanks to one grandfather's name, and another's red hair, and a shameless play for both of them since about age three. In fact—

TRACY. I never! I loved them!

SETH. —In fact, you have everything it takes to make a lovely woman except the one essential—an understanding heart. Without it, you might just as well be made of bronze.

TRACY. *(After a moment. Turns front)* That's an awful thing to say to anyone.

SETH. Indeed it is.

TRACY. *(Turns to him)* So I'm to blame for Tina Mara, am I?

SETH. If any blame attaches, to some extent I expect you are.

TRACY. You coward.

SETH. No.—But better to be one than a prig— and a perennial spinster, however many marriages.

MARGARET. Seth! That's too much.

SETH. I'm afraid it's not enough. *(Rises; crosses Left to MARGARET)* I'm afraid that nothing is.

TRACY. *(Is staring at him)* Wha-what did you say I was?

SETH. Do you want me to repeat it?

MARGARET. Seth—now I understand a great deal that I didn't.

SETH. *(Crossing to MARGARET)* It's all past now, Margaret. It has been for some time. Forgive me. You won't have to again. *I* understand a lot more than I did, as well. *(Pats shoulder. She touches his hand.)*

TRACY. "A prig and a—?" You mean—you mean you think *I* think I'm some kind of a virgin goddess or something?

SETH. *(Crossing Left Center)* If your ego wishes to call it that, yes.—Also, you've been talking like a jealous woman.

TRACY. *(Right Center)* A—? *(Turns away to Right, her face a study)* What's the matter with everyone all at once, anyhow? *(Goes to column Right.)*

UNCLE WILLIE. *(Comes in from Right 1. Crossing up Center)* Miss Imbrie preferred dressing, to my company. *(To SETH)* What do you make of that, Uncle Willie?

SETH. *(Crossing in Center)* We're going to drop all this. From now on you're yourself again—and so am I. I shall tell them we know what their tender mission is, and at the first opportunity.

(SANDY *and* DINAH *enter Left Center. He goes to back of table.*)

UNCLE WILLIE. *(Crossing back of table)* It's a pity. It was jolly good fun. Let's have a drink—

SANDY. *(Crossing back of table)* Damme, let's do that. *(Pours cocktails.)*

DINAH. *(Crossing down Right Center)* We're all so completely commonplace. *I* don't see how we interest anyone.

MARGARET. *(Rises, crossing to DINAH Right Center)* I think that dress hikes up a little behind.

DINAH. No—it's me that does.

(MARGARET *sits Right of Center table.* SANDY *pours two glasses of champagne.*)

TRACY. You look adorable, Dinah.

DINAH. Oh, thanks, Tracy! Thanks ever so much!

SANDY. A wedding without ushers and bridesmaids. Peace! It's wonderful—

DINAH. *(Crossing in to Left of MARGARET) I'm* the bridesmaid!—So can I have a cocktail at last? Can I?

MARGARET. Certainly not.

DINAH. It's a dirty gyp. *(Goes over to chaise and sits.)*

SANDY. Tracy? *(Goes to her with cocktail. She shakes her head)* Champagne, instead?

TRACY. No, thanks.

SANDY. Excuse, please. I forgot, you never. *(Puts drink down on table.)*

UNCLE WILLIE. Never? The girl's demented.

TRACY. —But prigs don't.

UNCLE WILLIE. What's that?
TRACY. Nor spinsters.
SANDY. We don't get you.
TRACY. Nor goddesses, virgin or otherwise.

(MIKE *and* LIZ, *dressed for dinner, enter from Left
   Center.* SANDY *greets them as they come down
   Left Center.* LIZ *goes down Left.* MIKE *stays
   up Left.*)

SANDY. *(To* WILLIE) —Not completely: just a
borderline case. Hello, you were quick. *(Goes down
Right.)*

(TRACY, *over Right, noticing nothing, stares upstage.*)

UNCLE WILLIE. Miss Imbrie, you are a dream of
loveliness. A cocktail or champagne?
LIZ. *(Down Left)* Thanks, champagne. I've never
had enough.

(SETH *offers her his seat. She declines. He sits.*)

SANDY. *(Right)* You will tonight.

(WILLIE *gives them each a glass.*)

MIKE. *(Up L e f t)*   SETH. *(Simultaneous-*
Champagne flew, *(To*   *ly)* Mr. Connor—oh—
WILLIE)* Mr. Lord—er   excuse me—
—that is to say—
MIKE. *(To* WILLIE) Mr. Lord, Miss Imbrie and
I have something on our minds—
UNCLE WILLIE. *(Back of Center table)* That's
splendid; just the place for it. What?
MIKE. Well—er—it's rather hard to explain—it's
—er—about the reason we're here and so forth.

SETH. I think perhaps there's something I ought to explain too—

MIKE. But did you ever hear of a man named Sidney Kidd—

(THOMAS, *the butler, enters Left with a tray and note and comes to foot of chaise.*)

SETH. —And did you ever hear of a man named Seth—er—? What is it, Thomas?

THOMAS. They've just phoned a telegram, Mr. Lord—

UNCLE WILLIE. Give it here.

THOMAS. It's for Mrs. Lord, Mr. Tracy.

(LIZ *and* MIKE *look.*)

UNCLE WILLIE. Then why didn't you say so?

THOMAS. Mrs. Lord and Miss Lord, that is.

MARGARET. Read it, Thomas. I haven't my glasses.

SANDY. *(Right Center)* Hey! Wait a minute!

MARGARET. Read it, Thomas.

THOMAS. *(Left)* "Most frightfully sorry will not be able to get down for the wedding as am confined to my bed with everything wrong. Baby better. It was only gas. Love, Father." Is there any answer, Madam?

MARGARET. No, Thomas—none in this world.

(THOMAS *goes out Left.*)

LIZ. *(To* WILLIE*)* He got a little mixed up, didn't he?

UNCLE WILLIE. A common mistake.

SETH. Now do you understand, Mr. Connor?

MIKE. I think we do.

LIZ. It's wonderful. Lord only knows where we go from here.

SANDY. To Aunt Geneva's!— Come on, everybody.

DINAH. *(Rising from chair—upstage end)* My first party, and about time.

UNCLE WILLIE. *(Going to* LIZ, *over her shoullder, speaks)* Who'll come in my little car with me?

MARGARET. *(Cutting in and separating him from* LIZ*)* Seth and Dinah and I.—Sandy, will you bring Miss Imbrie and Mr. Connor?

SANDY. *(Gets up Center. Crossing to* LIZ*)* Like a shot.

DINAH. The evening is pregnant with possibilities.

MARGARET. *(Takes her gently by shoulders and ushers her out door Left)* "Full of" is better, dear.
                                        (WARN Curtain.)

(SETH *goes to door Left.* WILLIE *starts to cross* Left *but hesitates long enough in passing to pinch* LIZ *behind, then goes out innocently.)*

LIZ. *(Jumps forward slightly)* Ouch!

(SETH, *who had been on his way out Left, stops; comes to* LIZ.*)*

SETH. What was it?

LIZ. N-nothing. (SETH *goes out. She turns to* SANDY *on her Right)* You know, I felt exactly as if I'd been pinched.

SANDY. Don't think you weren't. *(They both go out Left.)*

(MIKE *crosses down Center; sees* TRACY; *doesn't intend to follow.)*

MIKE. Aren't you coming?

TRACY. *(Down Right)* I'll follow along with George.

MIKE. What's the matter with you, Tracy? *(Below table.)*

TRACY. You tell *me*, will you?

MIKE. *(Looks at her intently)* Damn if I know. I'd like to.

TRACY. *(Smiles uncertainly)* Well, if you happen to find out—

MIKE. —I'll tell you. Sure.

TRACY. —And remember, Mike—"With the Rich and Mighty"—

MIKE. "Always a little Patience"—Yes, Highness. I will.

TRACY. Do that. Please do.—

(He goes out Left. She stands for a second, then comes to table, pours a glass of champagne and drinks. Starts to pour a second as the—)

CURTAIN FALLS

ACT TWO

SCENE II

The porch. About half-past five on Saturday morning. It is going to be a clear day, and throughout the scene the light increases. MAC, the night watchman, about thirty, crosses the path from Left 1 to Right 1, smoking a pipe and swinging a lighted lantern. He goes out Right. SANDY enters Right Center from the house. He is carrying a tray with two bottles of champagne, one already opened, a pitcher of milk, and glasses. He is followed by TRACY. BOTH are in evening dress.

SANDY. *(At back of table)* The question is, can we get away with it?

TRACY. *(Crossing Left of him)* You've got to get away with it! You must, Sandy!

SANDY. Me? It's your idea, not mine.

TRACY. *(Gets glass champagne)* What difference does that make? *(Back of table Center.)*

SANDY. You get the ideas and I do all the work.

TRACY. Sandy!

SANDY. Okay. *(Goes to chair Right of table.)*

TRACY. What you don't already know about the great Sidney Kidd, you can certainly fill in from Mike's ravings tonight.

SANDY. *(Sits)* I used to have that *Dime* lingo down pretty pat.

TRACY. *(Crossing Right of him—kneels at his knee)* It's a chance to write a beauty; you know it is.

SANDY. Then I swap it with Kidd for Connor's piece on us—and where am I?

TRACY. You'll have the satisfaction of knowing you saved the lot of us single-handed.

SANDY. And if he won't swap?

TRACY. I'm not worried about that.

SANDY. I suppose there's a fair chance the *Post* would go for it.

TRACY. Of course! You can't possibly lose. Quick —they'll be here! How long will it take you? *(Rises and drinks.)*

SANDY. *(Rises)* Three thousand words—all night —what there's left of it. *(Looks at his watch)* Holy cats! You get to bed.

TRACY. *(Right Center)* Have you got a typewriter?

SANDY. *(Right Center)* My old Corona is upstairs, I think.

TRACY. Make it smoke.

SANDY. You bet.

TRACY. Suds. I can't stand it. You won't fall asleep?

SANDY. I've drunk nothing but black coffee since Connor began his lecture.

TRACY. "Sidney Kidd—his habits—his habitat and how to hunt him."

SANDY. Poor Connor! It must have been bottled up in him for years.

TRACY. Waiter, another bottle.

SANDY. *(Crossing Left Center and turning)* No. I've got enough for three articles now. Profile—fullface—

TRACY. *(Crossing below table)* —Also rear elevation.—Mike and Liz—they mustn't suspect, Sandy.

SANDY. Oh no— oh my, no!

TRACY. *(Pours drink.)* They have simply stepped in their own chewing gum.—I suppose Kidd has one of those private numbers the rich and the mighty hide behind in New York. *(Gets Right Center.)*

SANDY. I'll dig it out of Liz and give him a buzz.

TRACY. *(Right of table)* What will you say?

SANDY. I'll be brief, bluff, belligerent. (TRACY *laughs; pours herself a glass of champagne)* Hey—lay off that!

TRACY. Why?

SANDY. *(Front of table)* You are already in wine, sister.

TRACY. Me? You lie. It never affects me, not in the slightest.

SANDY. That's because you never take it.

TRACY. Even if I did, it wouldn't.

SANDY. Don't say that: it's unlucky. *(Shakes his head over her)* I have seen people fly in the face of Pommery before.

TRACY. *(Crossing down over Right; sits on steps)* I've just got a good head, I guess.

SANDY. *(Crossing down with her)* Don't say it, don't say it!

TRACY. Sandy, you fool—

SANDY. George will spank.

TRACY. I could spank George for the way he behaved.

SANDY. *(Sits)* He had a right to be sore. You and Connor were gone for two hours, at least.

TRACY. You were along.

SANDY. All the same, tongues were wagging like tails. George said—

TRACY. George wanted to leave sharp at twelve—how could we?

SANDY. They need a lot of sleep, those big fellows.

TRACY. They must.—Then at one, with Father and Mother and Dinah.—Then at two, then at three—every hour on the hour. We fought like wolves in the car coming home.

SANDY. I hope you explained.

TRACY. Certainly not. He should have known. He was extremely rude. You'd have thought I had been out with Dexter, *(A pause)* —I wonder where Dext was? I half expected him to— I don't like the look behind Dexter's eyes, Sandy. It makes me sad.

SANDY. Don't be sad, Tracy. *(His arms about her shoulder.)*

TRACY. Oh, Sandy, if you knew how I envy you and Sue that darling fat creature you've just produced—

SANDY. You'll probably have four or five of your own any day now.

TRACY. Six! Oh, I hope—I do hope—I hope I'm good for something besides knocking out golf balls and putting horses over fences.

SANDY. You're good for my money any day.

TRACY. Thanks! *(Rises, crossing Center)* Was I really mean to George, I wonder? I don't want to be.

SANDY. You're in an odd mood, little fellah. What's amiss—what's afoot?

TRACY. *(Down on ground Center)* I guess it's just that—a lot of things I always thought were terribly important I find now are—and the other way around—and—oh, what the hell. *(Goes up step and to table with glass.)*

SANDY. *(Rises—crossing up to her at table)* I don't think I'd spend much more time with Connor tonight, if I were you.

TRACY. *(Left of table)* Why not?

SANDY. *(Front of table)* Writers with wine sauce intoxicate little girls.

TRACY. *(Laughs uncertainly. Sits on front of table)* They sort of do, don't they?—He fascinates me. He's so violent, Sandy.

SANDY. *(Sits Right of her)* He's fallen, Tray. I could hear him bump.

TRACY. *(Rises)* Mind your own beeswax, old Nosey Parker.

SANDY. Get thee to bed.

(She reaches for glass—he takes it from her hand.)

TRACY. No!

SANDY. *(He puts glass down)* —Before you have to be carried.

TRACY. No! No! No! *(Throws up her arms and head back; crosses over Right)* I feel too delicious! Sandy, I feel just elegant. *(Cocks her head, listening up Right)* Is that my bedroom telephone?

SANDY. Now you're hearing things.

TRACY. It couldn't be anyone but George. I *was* sort of swinish to him. Perhaps I'd better— *(Starts up Right)* As for you—get to work, you dog. Stop leaning on your shovel. *(She sees MIKE coming into the porch from Left. He is in fine fettle. Goes Center, back of table. Pours champagne. SANDY goes Right.)*

MIKE. Listen! Now I'm really under way. Miss not an inflection.

TRACY. Is it Connor the poet, or Connor the conspirator?

MIKE. Both! *(Pours himself a glass of wine)* "No lightweight is balding, battlebrowed Sidney Kidd, no mean displacement, his: for windy bias, bicarbonate." *(Drinks the wine; looks at the glass)* That is funny stuff. I'm used to whiskey. Whisky is a clap on the back. Champagne, entwining arms.

TRACY. *(Crossing Left, back of MIKE)* That's pretty. Is it poetry? *(On arm of chair Left of table.)*

MIKE. *Dime* will tell.

SANDY. "None before him but Writer Wolfgang Goethe has known all about all. Gigantic was Goethe's output, bigger already is Kidd's. Sample from his own pen: 'Pittsburgh is a gentle city.'"

TRACY. Sidney is a gentle man.

(MIKE and TRACY look at each other.)

MIKE. Potent, able, beady-eyed scion of great wealth in Quakertown, why don't you do a piece on our great and good friend?

SANDY. *(Right)* On Kidd?

MIKE. *(Center)* On none other.

SANDY. Nimble scrivener, it's an idea.

TRACY. Brilliant. I wish *I'd* thought of it.

MIKE. Baby Giant Tycooness.

TRACY. But would it not be a low, dirty deed?

MIKE. *He'd* print a scandal about his best friend: he's said he would.

SANDY. Who is his best friend?

MIKE. I guess Santa Claus. *(Crossing Left)* What is this mist before my eyes?

TRACY. *(Rises and goes to Left of table)* I tell you what: let's all have a quick swim to brighten us up. Go get Liz, Sandy. *(Takes off her bracelet and two rings and leaves them on table.)*

SANDY. Not me; it's too cold this early.

TRACY. It's the best hour of the day! Dexter and I always swam after parties.

MIKE. *(Over Left Center)* I haven't got any bathing suit.

TRACY. But we won't need any! It's just ourselves. *(Turns to him and after a short pause he goes back of table—pours two drinks of champagne.)*

MIKE. Let's dip into this instead. *(Pours more champagne.)*

TRACY. *(After a brief pause, to SANDY)* No takers. —Get Liz anyway, Sandy.

SANDY. If she's not in bed— Or even if she is. *(Goes out Right Center.)*

TRACY. *(Looking at MIKE)* That was an odd thing you just did—

MIKE. Me? *(Crosses down front of Right chair with drink.)*

TRACY. *(In front of table)* You. For a moment you made me—self-conscious.

MIKE. How? About what?

TRACY. Never mind. *(Raises her glass)* Hello, you.

MIKE. *(Raises his)* Hello.

TRACY. You look fine.

MIKE. I *feel* fine.

TRACY. Quite a fellah.

MIKE. They say.

(They drink.)

TRACY. Did you enjoy the party?

MIKE. Sure. The prettiest sight in this fine, pretty world is the Privileged Class enjoying its privileges. *(Drinks.)*

TRACY. *(Crossing down lower stage Left)* —Also somewhat of a snob.

MIKE. How do you mean?

TRACY. I'm wondering.

MIKE. *(Leaves glass on table)* Consider, Gentle Reader, they toil not, neither do they spin.

TRACY. Oh, yes, they do! They spin in circles. *(Spins and sits on floor over Left.)*

MIKE. *(Crosses down to her)* Nicely put. "Awash with champagne was Mrs. Willie Q. Tracy (born Geneva Biddle)'s stately pleasure dome on a hill-top in smart Radnor, P.A. on a Saturday night late in June; the eve of her great-niece's—" *(Sits beside her)* —Tracy, you can't marry that guy. *(She leaves glass on floor near foot of chaise.)*

TRACY. George?—I'm going to. Why not?

MIKE. I don't know; I'd have thought I'd be for it, but somehow you just don't seem to match up.

TRACY. Then the fault's with me.

MIKE. Maybe so; all the same you can't do it.

TRACY. *(Rising)* No? Come around about noon tomorrow—I mean today. *(Goes Center.)*

MIKE. *(Rises, after a pause)* Tracy—

TRACY. Yes, Mr. Connor?

MIKE. How do you mean, I'm "a snob"?

TRACY. You're the worst kind there is: an intellectual snob. You've made up your mind awfully young, it seems to me.

MIKE. *(Crossing to her, Center)* Thirty's about time to make up your mind.—And I'm nothing of the sort, not Mr. Connor.

TRACY. The time to make up your mind about people, is never. Yes, you are—and a complete one.

MIKE. You're quite a girl.

TRACY. You think?

MIKE. I know.

TRACY. Thank you, Professor. I don't think I'm exceptional.

MIKE. You are, though.

TRACY. I know any number like me. You ought to get around more.

MIKE. In the Upper Clahss? No, thanks.

TRACY. You're just a mass of prejudices, aren't

you? You're so much thought and so little feeling, Professor. *(Goes Right.)*

MIKE. Oh, I am, am I?

TRACY. Yes, you am, are you! *(Stops and turns on him)* Your damned intolerance furiates me. I mean *in*furiates me. I should think, of all people, a writer would need tolerance. The fact is, you'll never —you can't be a first-rate writer or a first-rate human being until you learn to have some small regard for— *(Suddenly she stops. Her eyes widen, remembering. She turns from him)* Aren't the geraniums pretty, Professor? *(Crossing extreme Right)* Is it not a handsome day that begins?

MIKE. *(Gets up on upper platform)* Lay off that "Professor."

TRACY. Yes, Professor. *(Up on platform.)*

MIKE. *(Right Center)* You've got all the arrogance of your class, all right, haven't you?

TRACY. *(Right)* Holy suds, what have "classes" to do with it?

MIKE. Quite a lot.

TRACY. Why? What do they matter—except for the people in them? George comes from the so-called "lower" class, Dexter comes from the upper. Well?

MIKE. Well?

TRACY. —Though there's a great deal to be said for Dexter—and don't you forget it! *(Goes Center.)*

MIKE. I'll try not to.

TRACY. *(Crossing above table to over Left for glass)* Mac, the night-watchman, is a prince among men and Joey, the stable-boy, is a rat. Uncle Hugh is a saint. Uncle Willie's a pincher. *(Picks up glass.)*

MIKE. So what?

TRACY. *(Crossing to table—pours)* There aren't any rules about human beings, that's all!—You're teaching me things, Professor; this is new to me. Thanks, I am beholden to you. *(Pours drink.)*

MIKE. *(Watching her)* Not at all.

TRACY. *(Gets below table)* "Upper" and "lower," my eye! I'll take the lower, thanks. *(Starts to drink.)*

MIKE. *(Over Right)* —If you can't get a drawing-room.

TRACY. *(Stops drinking and holds. Turns)* What do you mean by that?

MIKE. *(Crossing in Right)* My mistake.

TRACY. Decidedly.

MIKE. *(Crossing a bit Right)* Okay.

TRACY. You're insulting.

MIKE. *(Near post)* I'm sorry.

TRACY. *(Leaning on table)* Oh, don't apologize!

MIKE. *(At Right post)* Who the hell's apologizing?

TRACY. *(Puts glass on table)* I never knew such a man.

MIKE. You wouldn't be likely to, dear—not from where *you* sit.

TRACY. Talk about arrogance! *(Turning up at table.)*

MIKE. *(Weakening)* Tracy— *(Crossing in Center, over her shoulder.)*

TRACY. What do you want?

MIKE. You're wonderful.

TRACY. *(She horse laughs; her back to him)* Professor—may I go out?

MIKE. Class is dismissed. *(She moves Left)* Miss Lord *(She stands still)* will please wait.

TRACY. Miss Lord is privileged. *(Turns and meets his gaze. Goes to him.)*

MIKE. There's magnificence in you, Tracy. I'm telling you.

TRACY. I'm—! *(A moment. Crossing below him to Right)* Now I'm getting self-conscious again. I —it's funny— *(Another moment. Then)* Mike, let's— *(Turns to him.)*

MIKE. What?

urns front and to Right) I—I don't
p, I guess. It's late.

-A magnificence that comes out of your
; in your voice, in the way you stand there,
y you walk. You're lit from within, bright,
right. There are fires banked down in you,
hearu. ires and holocausts—

TRACY. *(Turns to him)* You—I don't seem to you
—made of bronze, then—

MIKE. *(Step to her)* You're made of flesh and
blood—that's the blank, unholy surprise of it. You're
the golden girl, Tracy, full of love and warmth and
delight— What the hell's this? You've got tears in
your eyes.

TRACY. *(Right Center)* Shut up, shut up!—Oh,
Mike—keep talking—keep talking! *Talk,* will you?

MIKE. I've stopped.

*(For a long moment they look at each other. Then
TRACY speaks, deliberately, harshly.)*

TRACY. Why? Has your mind taken hold again,
dear Professor?

MIKE. You think so?

TRACY. *(Crossing Right)* Yes, Professor.

MIKE. A good thing, don't you agree?

TRACY. *(Leaning against post Right)* No, Professor.

MIKE. Drop that Professor—you hear me?

TRACY. Yes, Professor.

MIKE. *(Slowly crossing in to her over Right)*
That's really all I am to you, is it?

TRACY. Of course, Professor.

MIKE. Are you sure?

TRACY. *(Looks up at him)* Why, why, yes—yes,
of course, Profess— *(His kiss stops the word. The
kiss is taken and returned. After it she exclaims
softly)* Golly. *(She gazes at him wonderingly, then*

raises her face to receive another. Then she stands in his arms, her cheek against his breast, amazement in her eyes) Golly Moses.

MIKE. Tracy dear—

TRACY. Mr. Connor—Mr. Connor—

MIKE. Let me tell you something—

TRACY. No, don't— All of a sudden I've got the shakes.

MIKE. I have, too.

TRACY. What *is* it?

MIKE. It must be something like love.

TRACY. No, no! It mustn't be. It can't—

MIKE. Why? Would it be inconvenient?

TRACY. Terribly. Anyway, it isn't. I know it's not. Oh, Mike, I'm a bad girl—

MIKE. Not you.

TRACY. We're out of our minds.

MIKE. —Right into our hearts.

TRACY. That ought to have music.

MIKE. It has, hasn't it?—Tracy, you lovely— *(Starts to kiss. She breaks embrace.)*

(She hears something; looks quickly toward the door Left.)

TRACY. *(Crossing Center, looking Left)* They're coming.

MIKE. The hell—

TRACY. *(Turns to him)* It's—it's not far to the pool. It's only over the lawn, in the birch-grove —it'll be lovely now.

MIKE. *(Holds his arm out)* Come on—

TRACY. Oh, it's as—it's as if my insteps—were melting away. —What is it? Have I—have I got feet of clay, or something?

MIKE. —Quick! Here they are— *(He takes her hand and hurries her down the steps.)*

TRACY. I—I feel so small! all at once.

MIKE. You're immense—you're tremendous.

TRACY. Not me—oh, not me! Put me in your pocket, Mike—

(They are gone—off Right 1.)

LIZ. *(Off Left)* You give those back!

(A moment, then SANDY *comes quickly in Left from the house, a sheaf of small photographs in his hand. He is followed by* LIZ, *in pajamas and wrapper.)*

SANDY. Look, Tracy— *(Sees that the porch is empty.)*

LIZ. *(Crossing down Left Center)* May I have them, please?

SANDY. Did Kidd *know* you took these shots of him?

LIZ. *(Crossing below table to Right)* Some of them.

SANDY. Sit down. Have a drink.

LIZ. I should say not. A drink would be redundant, tautological, and a mistake. *(Wearily she drops into chair Right of table and eyes the pitcher on the table)* Is that milk?

SANDY. *(Goes back of table)* That is milk.

LIZ. Gimme. Milk I will accept. *(He pours and gives her a glass)* I met this cow this afternoon. Nice Bossy.

SANDY. Let me keep just these three shots.

LIZ. What for?

SANDY. A low purpose.

LIZ. Sufficiently low?

SANDY. Nefarious.

LIZ. You won't reproduce them?

SANDY. Nope.

LIZ. Nor cause them to be reproduced?

SANDY. Honest.

LIZ. In any way, shape or manner, without permission?

SANDY. So help me, Sidney Kidd.

LIZ. Amen.

SANDY. What's his private number?

LIZ. You mean his private number or his **sacred** private number?

SANDY. The one by the bed and the bathtub.

LIZ. Regent 4-1416— *(Settles lower in the chair.* SANDY *goes to the telephone off Right Center)* I won't tell you. *(He dials one number)* Is Mr. Kittredge pure gold, Lord?

SANDY. *(Coming in doorway—but goes back into room again)* We must never doubt that, Missy.

LIZ. *(Sleepily) Lèse majesté*—excuse it, please.

SANDY. *(Comes in to doorway)* Regent 4-1416 New York. —Wayne—22-23. *(To* LIZ*)* —And Mr. Connor—what of him?

LIZ. Percentage of base metal. Alloy.

SANDY. So.

LIZ. —Which imparts a certain shape and firmness.

SANDY. *(In doorway)* Hello?—Mr. Kidd? This is Alexander Lord.

LIZ. *(Listens intently. Calling)* I know nothing about this.

SANDY. *(In doorway)* No, I'm in Philadelphia.— Yes, I know it is. It's early here, too. Look, Mr. Kidd, I think you'd better get over here as fast as you can. What?—I'm sorry to have to tell you, sir, but Connor has had an accident—yes, pretty bad— he had a pretty bad fall.— No, it's his heart we're worried about now.—Yes, I'm afraid so: He keeps talking about you, calling you names—I mean calling your name.—How's that?—No, the eleven o'clock's time enough. We don't expect him to regain consciousness much before then.

Liz. His only hope is to get fired—I know it is.

Sandy. Sorry, Miss Imbrie's sleeping. Shock.— *(Crossing into room)* The newspapers? No, they don't know a thing about it. I understand. What? I said I understood, didn't I?—Twelve twenty North Philadelphia—I'll have you met. *(Hangs up—puts the phone in place—enters porch)* He wants no publicity. *(Goes down Right.)*

Liz. *(Has suppressed her broadening grin. She stirs lazily in her chair and inquires)* Who was that?

Sandy. God.

(She looks toward the garden path. Dexter whistles off Right.)

Liz. Do I hear someone?

Sandy. *(Looks—crossing down Right)* It's Mac, the night-watchman. —Liz—you're in love with Connor, aren't you?

Liz. People ask the oddest questions.

(Dexter, whistling, enters Right 1, smoking cigarette.)

Sandy. Why don't you marry him?

Liz. I can't hear you.

Sandy. I say, why don't you—? *(Dexter comes along the path and stops at the steps Right)* Hello, here's an early one!

Dexter. Hello. I saw quite a full day ahead, and got myself up. *(He seats himself on step Right)* —A good party?

Sandy. Fine.

Dexter. Good.

Liz. *(Rises)* —And sufficient. Hell or high water, I'm going to bed. *(Gets up Right and starts Left to back of table.)*

Sandy. *(Crossing up Right)* Why don't you, Liz —*you* know—what I asked?

Liz. *(Back of table)* He's still got a lot to learn,

and I don't want to get in his way yet a while. Okay?

SANDY. Okay.—Risky, though. Suppose another girl came along in the meantime?

LIZ. *(Up Left Center at door)* Oh, I'd just scratch her eyes out, I guess.—That is, unless she was going to marry someone else the next day. *(In doorway.)*

SANDY. You're a good number, Liz.

LIZ. No, I just photograph well. *(Goes out Left Center.)*

DEXTER. *(Over Right)* Complications?

SANDY. *(Back of table, looking at pictures he brought on)* There might be.

DEXTER. Where are they?

SANDY. Who?

DEXTER. The complications.

SANDY. They went up—at least I hope and pray that they did.

DEXTER. Well, well.

SANDY. *(Moves toward the door Left)* Make yourself comfortable, Dext. I've got a little black-mailing to do. (SANDY *goes out Left.*)

(A pause as DEXTER *smokes. He sees someone coming Left 1. Rises and stamps out cigarette.* GEORGE *comes up the Left 1 path and mounts the porch. He is still in evening clothes.)*

GEORGE. *(Entering)* What are you doing here?

DEXTER. *(Crossing Center)* Oh, I'm a friend of the family's—just dropped in for a chat.

GEORGE. Don't try to be funny. I asked you a question.

DEXTER. I might ask you the same one.

GEORGE. I telephoned Tracy and her phone didn't answer.

DEXTER. I didn't telephone. I just came right over.

GEORGE. I was worried, so I—

DEXTER. Yes, I was worried, too.

GEORGE. About what?

DEXTER. *(Crossing Left, face to face with* GEORGE*)* What do you think of this Connor—or do you?

GEORGE. What about him?

DEXTER. I just wondered.

GEORGE. Listen: if you're trying to insinuate some—

DEXTER. My dear fellow, I wouldn't dream of it! I was only— *(Goes up to table—sees jewelry.)*

GEORGE. Who's that I hear? *(Goes to Right; looks off.)*

DEXTER. *(He finds the ring and bracelet upon the table. He glances quickly in the direction of the swimming pool, then pockets them)* Look, Kittredge: I advise you to go to bed.

GEORGE. *(Crossing Center)* Oh, you do, do you?

DEXTER. *(Above* GEORGE*)* Yes. I strongly urge you to do so at once.

GEORGE. *(Crossing Left, facing upstage)* I'm staying right here.

DEXTER. *(Looks at him)* You're making a mistake. Somehow I don't think you'll understand.

GEORGE. You'd better leave that to—! I hear someone walking— *(Looks off up Right.)*

DEXTER. Yes?—Must be Mac. *(Crossing up Right, he calls out)* It's all right, Mac—it's only us! *(Turns to* GEORGE—*comes down to him)* Come on—I'll walk along with you.

GEORGE. *(Crossing up on porch at table)* I'm staying right here—so are you.

DEXTER. All right, then: take the works, and may God be with you. *(Retires to over Left.)*

(Finally MIKE *appears from Right 1, comes to Right corner of the porch, carrying* TRACY *in his arms.* BOTH *are in bathrobes and slippers and there is a jumble of clothes, his and hers, slung*

over MIKE's *shoulder. He stops with her for a moment at the top of the steps. She stirs in his arms, speaks lowly, as if from a long way away. As they enter* DEXTER *crosses below table to up Right.* GEORGE *goes above to Right; confronts* MIKE.*)*

TRACY. Take me upstairs, Mike—
MIKE. Yes, dear. Here we go.
GEORGE. *(Up Center)* What the—!
DEXTER. *(Comes swiftly in between him and* MIKE*)* Easy, old boy! *(To* MIKE*)* She's not hurt?
MIKE. No. She's just—
TRACY. *(Murmurs dreamily)* Not wounded, Sire —but dead.
GEORGE. She—she hasn't any clothes on!
TRACY. *(Into* MIKE's *shoulder)* Not a stitch—it's delicious.
MIKE. *(Speaks lowly)* It seems the minute she hit the water, the wine—
DEXTER. *(Glances at* GEORGE, *who can only stare)* A likely story, Connor.
MIKE. What did you say?
DEXTER. I said, a likely story!
MIKE. Listen: if—!
DEXTER. You'll come down again directly?
MIKE. Yes, if you want.
DEXTER. I want.
TRACY. *(Lifts her head limply and looks at them)* Hello, Dexter. Hello, George. *(Crooks her head around and looks vaguely up at* MIKE*)* Hello, Mike.

*(*DEXTER *goes and opens drapery Right Center.* MIKE *starts to take her off.)*

DEXTER. The second door on the right at the top of the stairs. Mind you don't wake Dinah.

*(*MIKE *moves toward the door with* TRACY.*)*

TRACY. My feet are of clay—made of clay—did you know it? *(Drops her head again and tightens her arms around* MIKE's *neck)* Goo' nigh'—sleep well, little man.

(MIKE *carries her out, past* DEXTER.)

DEXTER. *(Calling off)* Look out for Dinah. *(Crossing to front of table—sits on it)* How are the mighty fallen! (GEORGE *goes below to Right)* —But if I know Tracy—and I know her very well—she'll remember very little of this. For the second time in her life, she may draw quite a tidy blank.—Of course she may worry, though—

GEORGE. Good God!

DEXTER. *(Turns on him swiftly. On edge of table)* You believe it, then?

GEORGE. Believe what?

DEXTER. The—er—the implications, of what you've seen, let's say.

GEORGE. *(Crossing in a bit)* What else is there to believe?

DEXTER. Why, I suppose that's entirely up to you.

GEORGE. I've got eyes, and I've got imagination, haven't I?

DEXTER. I don't know. Have you?

GEORGE. *(Crossing in Right Center)* So you pretend not to believe it—

DEXTER. Yes, I pretend not to.

GEORGE. Then you don't know women. *(Goes in Center to* DEXTER.)

DEXTER. Possibly not.

GEORGE. You're a blind fool!

DEXTER. Oh, quite possibly!

GEORGE. *(Crossing below him to up Left)* —God!

DEXTER. *(Studies him)* You won't be too hard on her, will you?

GEORGE. I'll make up my own mind what I'll be!

DEXTEP. But we're all only human, you know. *(Goes Left and up Center.)*   *(WARN Curtain.)*

GEORGE. You—all of you—with your damned sophisticated ideas!

DEXTER. *(Up Center, back of table)* Isn't it hell?

(MIKE *comes swiftly through the Right Center door and up to* DEXTER.)

MIKE. Well?

GEORGE. *(Crossing up and over* R.*)* Why, you low-down—!

DEXTER. *(Quickly)* The lady is my wife, Mr. Connor. *(His upper cut to* MIKE'S *jaw sends him across the porch and to the floor down Right.)*

GEORGE. You!—What right have—? *(Goes over Right.)*

DEXTER. —A husband's, till tomorrow, Kittredge.

GEORGE. I'll make up my mind, all right! *(He turns and storms out Left 1.)*

DEXTER. *(Bends over* MIKE. *After* GEORGE *is gone)* Okay, old man?

MIKE. *(Sits up, nursing his chin)* Listen: if you think—!

DEXTER. I know—I'm sorry. But I thought I'd better hit you before he did. (MAC, *the night watchman, comes along the garden path, Right 1)* Hello, Mac. How are you? *(Rises.)*

MAC. Hello, Dexter! Anything wrong?

DEXTER. Not a thing, Mac.—Just as quiet as a church.

MAC. Who is it? *(Looks at* MIKE, *who turns to face him)* Hell!—I thought it might be Kittredge.

DEXTER. We can't have everything, Mac.

(MAC *continues along the path to Left 1.)*

CURTAIN

ACT THREE

The sitting room. Late morning. Saturday. The room is full of bright noonday sun and there are flowers everywhere.

AT RISE: WILLIE, *in a morning coat, fancy waistcoat and Ascot, stands in the Center of the room, facing* THOMAS. WILLIE *is demanding impatiently.*

THOMAS. *(Right)* I am trying to think, Mr. Tracy.

UNCLE WILLIE. Well? Well?

THOMAS. She wakened late, sir, and had a tray in her room. I believe May and Elsie are just now dressing her.

UNCLE WILLIE. It's not the bride I'm asking about —it's her sister.

THOMAS. I haven't seen Miss Dinah since breakfast, sir. She came down rather early.

UNCLE WILLIE. Is there anything wrong with her?

THOMAS. I did notice that she seemed a trifle silent, took only one egg and neglected to finish her cereal. The hot-cakes and bacon, however, went much as usual.

UNCLE WILLIE. She was telephoning me like a mad woman before I was out of my tub. (DINAH, *in blue-jeans, slides in from Left 1 and up behind him*) I expected at least two bodies, hacked beyond recognition, the house stiff with police, and— (DINAH *touches his coat tail. He starts and turns*)

Good God, child—don't do that! I drank champagne last night.

DINAH. Hello, Uncle Willie.

UNCLE WILLIE. *Why* must I come on ahead of your Aunt Geneva? Why must I waste not one minute? What's amiss? What's about? Speak up! Don't stand there with your big eyes— (DINAH *nudges him, pointing toward* THOMAS*)* like a stuffed owl.

(DINAH *glances significantly at* THOMAS*.)*

THOMAS. Is there anything else, sir? If not—

UNCLE WILLIE. Thanks, Thomas, nothing.

(THOMAS *goes out Right 2*. DINAH *pulls at* WILLIE'S *coat-tail, drawing him to the armchair Left Center.)*

DINAH. Come over here—and speak very low. Nobody's allowed in this room this morning but Tracy—and speak terribly low. *(Puts him in chair.)*

UNCLE WILLIE. What the Sam Hill for? What's alack? What's afoot?

DINAH. I had no one to turn to but you, Uncle Willie.

UNCLE WILLIE. People are always turning to me. I wish they'd stop.

DINAH. It's desperate. It's about Tracy. *(Goes below table to Left and kneels in armchair; leans over table to* WILLIE*.)*

UNCLE WILLIE. Tracy? What's she up to now? Tracy this, and Tracy that. Upstairs and downstairs and in my lady's chamber.

DINAH. How did you know?

UNCLE WILLIE. Know what?

DINAH. It seems to me you know just about everything.

UNCLE WILLIE. I have a fund of information accumulated through the years. I am old, seasoned, and full of instruction. But there are gaps in my knowledge. Ask me about falconry, say, or ballistics, and you will get nowhere.

DINAH. I meant more about people and—and sin.

UNCLE WILLIE. I know only that they are inseparable. I also know that the one consolation for being old is the realization that, however you live, you will never die young.—Get to the point, child. What do you want of me?

DINAH. Advice.

UNCLE WILLIE. On what subject or subjects?

DINAH. Well, *(Crossing back of table)* lookit; you don't like George, do you?

UNCLE WILLIE. Kittredge? I deplore him.

DINAH. *(Between his armchair and table)* And you'd like it if Tracy didn't go ahead and have married him after all—or would you?

UNCLE WILLIE. Where do you go to school?

DINAH. I don't yet. I'm going some place next Fall.

UNCLE WILLIE. And high time.—Like it? I would cheer. I would raise my voice in song.

DINAH. Well, I think I know a way to stop her from, but I need advice on how.

UNCLE WILLIE. Proceed, child—proceed cautiously.

DINAH. Well, suppose she all of a sudden developed an illikit passion for someone—

UNCLE WILLIE. Can you arrange it?

DINAH. It doesn't need to be. It is already.

UNCLE WILLE. Ah? Since when?

DINAH. Last night—and well into the morning.

UNCLE WILLIE. You surprise me, Dinah.

DINAH. Imagine what *I* was—and just imagine what *George* would be.

UNCLE WILLIE. And—er—the object of this—er
—illikit passion—

DINAH. Let him be nameless. (WILLIE *is exasper-
ated*) —Only tell me, should I tell George?—It's
getting late.

*(Unnoticed by them, DEXTER has come in Left 2
and remains up by piano.)*

UNCLE WILLIE. Maybe he'll want to marry he
anyway.

DINAH. But she can't. If she marries anyone, it's
got to be Mr. Connor!

UNCLE WILLIE. Connor? Why Connor?

DINAH. She's just got to, that's all.

DEXTER. *(Crossing to Center)* Why, Dinah? What
makes you think she should?

DINAH. *(Looks at him, appalled. Follows to Center, Left of DEXTER)* Dexter—

DEXTER. Isn't that a pretty big order to swing at
this late date?

DINAH. I—I didn't say anything. What did *I* say?

DEXTER. Of course, you might talk it over with
her.—But maybe you have.

DINAH. Certainly not. I haven't!

UNCLE WILLIE. Apparently the little cherub has
seen or heard something.

DEXTER. That's Dexter's own Dinah.

UNCLE WILLIE. I must say *you* show a certain
amount of cheek, walking in here on this, of all
mornings.

DEXTER. Tracy just did a very sweet thing: she
telephoned and asked me what to do for a feeling
of fright accompanied by headache.

DINAH. I should think it would be bad luck for a
first husband to see the bride before the wedding.

DEXTER. *(Crossing, sits on arm of chair Right
Center)* That's what I figured.—Why all this about

Connor, Dinah? Did the party give you bad dreams?

DINAH. It wasn't any dream.

DEXTER. I wouldn't be too sure. Once you've gone to bed it's pretty hard to tell, isn't it?

DINAH. Is it?

DEXTER. You bet your hat it is. It's practically impossible.

DINAH. I thought it was Sandy's typewriter woke me up.

(TRACY *comes in from the hall, Right 2, in the dress in which she is to be married. She has a leather-strapped wrist-watch in her hand.* DEXTER *rises and goes up above sofa.* DINAH *to back of* WILLIE'S *chair, Left.)*

TRACY. *(Crossing down Right end of sofa)* Hello! Isn't it a fine day, though! Is everyone fine? That's fine! *(Crossing uncertainly Center of sofa. Sits)* My, I'm hearty.

DEXTER. How are you otherwise? *(Down to upper corner of sofa.)*

TRACY. I don't know what's the matter with me. I must have had too much sun yesterday.

DEXTER. It's awfully easy to get too much.

TRACY. My eyes don't open properly. *(Picks up silver cigarette box from coffee table; looks at eyes)* Please go home, Dext.

DEXTER. Not till we get those eyes open. *(Sits on sofa beside her.)*

TRACY. Uncle Willie, good morning.

UNCLE WILLIE. *(Leaning forward)* That remains to be seen.

TRACY. Aren't you here early?

UNCLE WILLIE. Weddings get me out like nothing else.

DINAH. It's nearly half-past twelve. *(Goes Right; sits armchair Right Center.)*

TRACY. It can't be!

DINAH. Maybe it can't, but it is.

TRACY. Where—where's Mother?

DINAH. *(Rises)* Do you want her?

TRACY. No, I just wondered.

DINAH. *(Reseats herself)* She's talking with the orchestra, and Father with the minister, and—

TRACY. Doctor Parsons—already?

DINAH. —And Miss Imbrie's gone with her camera to shoot the horses, and Sandy's in his room and—and Mr. Connor, he hasn't come down yet.

DEXTER. And it's Saturday.

TRACY. Thanks loads. It's nice to have things accounted for. *(Passes the hand with the wrist-watch over her eyes, then looks at the watch)* —Only I wonder what this might be?

DEXTER. It looks terribly like a wrist-watch.

TRACY. But whose? I found it in my room, I nearly stepped on it.

DINAH. Getting out of bed?

TRACY. Yes. Why?

DINAH. *(Knowingly)* I just wondered. *(Rises and crosses behind* WILLIE'S *chair, Left Center.)*

TRACY. *(Puts the watch on the table before her)* There's another mystery, Uncle Willie.

UNCLE WILLIE. Mysteries irritate me.

TRACY. I was robbed at your house last night.

UNCLE WILLIE. You don't say.

TRACY. Yes—my bracelet and my engagement ring are missing everywhere.

UNCLE WILLIE. Probably someone's house guest from New York.

(TRACY nods agreement.)

DEXTER *(Brings them from his pocket)* Here you are.

TRACY. *(Stares at them, then at him)* —But you weren't at the party!

DEXTER. Wasn't I?

TRACY. Were you?

DEXTER. Don't tell me you don't remember!

TRACY. I—I do now, sort of—but there were such a lot of people.

(DEXTER *gives jewels to her.* TRACY *puts them on table.)*

DEXTER. *(Rises, crossing up behind Right armchair)* You should have taken a quick swim to shake them off. There's nothing like a swim after a late night.

TRACY. —A swim. *(And her eyes grow rounder.)*

DEXTER. *(Laughs)* There! Now they're open!

DINAH. *(Crossing a bit to Center)* That was just the beginning—and it was no dream.

DEXTER. *(Glances at her, crossing to WILLIE)* Don't you think, sir, that if you and I went to the pantry at this point—you know: speaking of eye-openers?

UNCLE WILLIE. *(Rises and precedes him toward the porch L.1)* The only sane remark I've heard this morning. I know a formula that is said to pop the pennies off the eyelids of dead Irishmen. *(Exits Left 1.)*

DEXTER. *(Over Left; stops at table)* Oh, Dinah—if conversation drags, you might tell Tracy your dream. *(Exits Left 1.)*

TRACY. What did he say?

DINAH. *(Center)* Oh, nothing. *(Crossing in front of sofa. Puts arm on* TRACY's *shoulder)* Tray—I hate you to get married and go away.

TRACY. I'll miss you, darling. I'll miss all of you.

DINAH. We'll miss you, too.—It—it isn't like

when you married Dexter, and just moved down the road a ways

TRACY. I'll come back often. It's only Wilkes-Barre.

DINAH. It gripes me.

TRACY. Baby.

(There is another silence. Finally DINAH speaks:)

DINAH. *(Sits on upper arm of sofa)* You know I did have the funniest dream about you last night.

TRACY. Did you? What was it?

DINAH. It was terribly interesting, and—and awfully scarey, sort of—

TRACY. *(Rises; a step forward)* Do you like my dress, Dinah?

DINAH. Yes, ever so much.

TRACY. *(Rises too quickly, wavers a moment, steadies herself, then moves to the Left 1 door)* It feels awfully heavy.—You'd better rush and get ready yourself. *(Goes Center to Left.)*

(MARGARET enters Right 1.)

DINAH. You know me: I don't take a minute.

(VIOLINS off Right tune up.)

MARGARET. Turn around, Tracy. (TRACY *turns)* Yes, it looks lovely. *(Goes to Center.)*

TRACY. *(Left)* What's that—that scratching sound I hear?

MARGARET. *(Center)* The orchestra tuning. Yes— *(Crossing up Right)* I'm glad we decided against the blue one. Where's your father? You know, I feel completely impersonal about all this. I can't quite grasp it. Get dressed, Dinah. *(Goes out into the hall. Right 2.)*

TRACY. *(Over Left blinks into the sunlight from Left 1)* That sun is certainly bright all right, isn't it?

DINAH. It was up awfully early.

TRACY. Was it?

DINAH. *(Crossing Left Center)* Unless I dreamed that, too.—It's supposed to be the longest day of the year or something, isn't it?

TRACY. I wouldn't doubt it for a minute.

DINAH. It was all certainly pretty rooty-tooty. *(Sits Right of table Left.)*

TRACY. What was?

DINAH. My dream.

TRACY. *(Crossing below table to Center)* Dinah, you'll have to learn sooner or later that no one is interested in anyone else's dreams. *(Goes to above armchair Right and back of sofa.)*

DINAH. —I thought I got up and went over to the window and looked out across the lawn. And guess what I thought I saw coming over out of the woods?

TRACY. *(Back of sofa, then crossing down Right)* I haven't the faintest idea. A skunk?

DINAH. Well, sort of.—It was Mr. Connor.

TRACY. Mr. Connor? *(At lower end of sofa.)*

DINAH. Yes—with his both arms full of something. And guess what it turned out to be?

TRACY. What?

DINAH. You—and some clothes. (TRACY *turns slowly and looks at her)* Wasn't it funny? It was sort of like as if you were coming from the pool—

TRACY. *(Closes her eyes)* The pool.—I'm going crazy. I'm standing here solidly on my own two hands going crazy.—And then what? *(Goes below sofa to Right Center.)*

DINAH. Then I thought I heard something outside in the hall, and I went and opened my door a crack and there he was, still coming along with you, puffing like a steam engine. His wind can't be very good.

TRACY. And then what?— *(Goes in Center.)*

DINAH. And you were sort of crooning—

TRACY. I never crooned in my life!

DINAH. I guess it just sort of sounded like you were. Then he—guess what?

TRACY. I—couldn't possibly.

DINAH. Then he just sailed right into your room with you and—and that scared me so, that I just flew back to bed—or thought I did—and pulled the covers up over my head and layed there shaking and thinking; if *that's* the way it is, why doesn't she marry him instead of old George? And then I must have fallen even faster asleep, because the next thing I knew it was eight o'clock and the typewriter still going.

TRACY. Sandy—typewriter—

DINAH. *(Rises; kneels in chair)* So in a minute I got up and went to your door and peeked in, to make sure you were all right—and guess what?

TRACY. *(Agonized)* What?

DINAH. You were. He was gone by then.

TRACY. Gone? Of course he was gone—he was never there!

DINAH. I know, Tracy.

TRACY. Well! I should certainly hope you did! *(Goes over Right to armchair; sits.)*

DINAH. *(Rises, following* TRACY*)* I'm certainly glad I do, because if I didn't and if in a little while I heard Doctor Parsons saying, "If anyone knows any just cause or reason why these two should not be united in holy matrimony"—*I* just wouldn't know what to do.—And it was all only a dream. *(Goes up Center slowly to stool.)*

TRACY. Naturally!

DINAH. I know. Dexter said so, straight off.—But isn't it funny, though—

TRACY. *(Half turning)* Dexter!

DINAH. *(Crossing down Center to Left of* TRACY*)* Yes.—He said—

TRACY. *(Grabbing* DINAH'S *arm)* You told Dexter all that?

DINAH. Not a word. Not one single word.—But you know how quick he is.

TRACY. Dinah Lord—you little fiend; how can you—?

SETH. *(Enters from the hall Right 2. Back of sofa)* Tracy, the next time you marry, choose a different Man of God, will you? This one wears me out. *(Goes to the Right 1 door; looks in)* Good heavens!—Dinah! Get into your clothes! You look like a tramp. *(Is about to go out again Right 2.* TRACY'S *voice stops him.)*

DINAH. I'm going. *(Goes up to corner Right.)*

TRACY. Father.

SETH. *(Turns to her. Crossing down Center)* Yes, Tracy?

TRACY. I'm glad you came back. I'm glad you're here.

SETH. Thank you, child.

TRACY. I'm sorry—I'm truly sorry I'm a disappointment to you.

SETH. I never said that, daughter—and I never will. *(Looks at her for a moment, touches her arm, then turns abruptly and goes out Right 2)* Where's your mother? Where's George?

MIKE. *(Comes in from the porch Left 1. Crossing in front of table Left, puts out cigarette)* Good morning.

TRACY. Oh, hello!

MIKE. I was taking the air. I like it, but it doesn't like me.—Hello, Dinah.

DINAH. *(Step toward him to armchair Left Center)* How do you do?

TRACY. *(Right Center)* Did—did you have a good sleep?

MIKE. *(Crossing in Center to* TRACY*)* Wonderful. How about you?

TRACY. Marvelous. Have you ever seen a handsomer day?

MIKE. Never. What did it set you back?

*(*DINAH *moves down Center.)*

TRACY. I got it for nothing, for being a good girl.

MIKE. Good.

(There is a brief silence. They look at DINAH. *Finally:)*

DINAH. *(Crossing below sofa to door Right 1)* I'm going, don't worry.

TRACY. Why should you?

DINAH. *(Over Right at lower end of sofa; turns to them)* I guess you must have things you wish to discuss.

TRACY. "Things to—"? What are you talking about?

DINAH. Only remember, it's getting late. *(Gingerly she opens the Right 1 door a crack, and peers in)* Some of them are in already. My, they look solemn. *(Closes door, and moves toward the hall up Right 2)* I'll be ready when you are. *(Exits Right 2.)*

TRACY. *(Crossing Left)* She's always trying to make situations. *(Front of table.* MIKE *arm of Right Center chair; laughs)* —How's your work coming— are you doing us up brown?

MIKE. I've—somehow I've lost my angle.

TRACY. How do you mean, Mike?

MIKE. I've just got so damn tolerant all at once, I doubt if I'll ever be able to write another line.

TRACY. *(Laughs)* You are a fellah, Mike.

MIKE. Or the mug of this world: I don't know.

TRACY. When you're at work you ought to be doing, you'll soon see that tolerance— What's the matter with your chin?

MIKE. Does it show?

TRACY. A little. What happened?

MIKE. I guess I just stuck it out too far.

TRACY. —Into a door, in the dark?

MIKE. That's it. *(Rises, crossing in Left)* Are you —are *you* all right, Tracy?

TRACY. Me? Of course! Why shouldn't I be?

MIKE. That was a flock of wine we put away.

TRACY. *(Crossing below him to armchair Right Center)* I never felt better in my life.

MIKE. That's fine. That's just daisy.

TRACY. *(Sits in armchair Right Center)* I—I guess we're lucky both to have such good heads.

MIKE. Yes, I guess. *(Goes to near her.)*

TRACY. It must be awful for people who—you know—get up and make speeches or—or try to start a fight—or, you know—misbehave in general.

MIKE. It certainly must.

TRACY. It must be—some sort of hidden **weakness** coming out.

MIKE. Weakness? I'm not so sure of that. *(Chuckles.)*

TRACY. *(She imitates him. Rises, crossing Center to Left)* Anyhow, I had a simply wonderful evening. I hope you enjoyed it too.

MIKE. *(Right Center)* I enjoyed the last part of it.

TRACY. *(Turns to him)* Really? Why?—why especially the last?

MIKE. Are you asking me, Tracy?

TRACY. *(Front of armchair Left Center)* Oh, you mean the swim!—We did swim, and so forth, didn't we?

MIKE. We swam, and so forth.

TRACY. *(Turns to him suddenly. At table Left Center)* Mike—

MIKE. *(Beside her)* You darling, darling girl—

TRACY. Mike!

MIKE. What can I say to you? Tell me, darling—

TRACY. *(Crossing below him to upper corner of sofa)* Not anything—don't say anything. And especially not "Darling."

MIKE. Never in this world will I ever forget you.

TRACY. —Not anything, I said.

MIKE. *(Crossing in back of armchair Right Center to her)* You're going to go through with it, then—

TRACY. Through with what?

MIKE. The wedding.

TRACY. Why—why shouldn't I?

MIKE. Well, you see, I've made a funny discovery: that in spite of the fact that someone's up from the bottom, he may be quite a heel. And that even though someone else's born to the purple, he still may be quite a guy.—Hell, I'm only saying what you said last night!

TRACY. I said a lot of things last night, it seems. *(Goes down.)*

MIKE. *(After a moment)* All right, no dice. But understand: also no regrets about last night.

TRACY. *(Backs away to Right)* Why should I have?

MIKE. *(Crossing below sofa to her)* That's it! That's the stuff; you're wonderful. You're aces, Tracy.

TRACY. *(Backing away from him to lower corner sofa)* You don't know what I mean! I'm asking you —tell me straight out—tell me the reason why I should have any— *(But she cannot finish. Her head drops)* No—don't.— *(Goes Center)* Just tell me— what time is it?

MIKE. *(Glancing at his wrist)* What's happened to my wrist watch?

TRACY. *(Stops, frozen; speaks without turning)* Why? Is it broken?

MIKE. *(Front of sofa)* It's gone. I've lost it somewhere.

TRACY. *(Left Center. After a moment)* I can't tell you how extremely sorry I am to hear that. *(Goes to table.)*

MIKE. Oh, well—I'd always just as soon not know the time.

TRACY. *(Her back to him)* There on the table—

MIKE. —What is? *(Goes to the coffee table; finds the watch)* Well, for the love of—! Who found it? I'll give a reward, or something. *(Straps the watch on his wrist.)*

TRACY. I don't think any reward will be expected.

DEXTER. *(Comes in Left 1, cocktail glass in hand)* Now, then! This medicine indicated in cases of— *(Stops at the sight of MIKE)* Hello, Connor. How are you?

MIKE. *(At sofa, crossing Left Center)* About as you'd think.—Is that for me?

DEXTER. *(Over Left)* For Tracy.—Why? Would you like one?

MIKE. *(Crossing to Left)* I would sell my grandmother for a drink—and you know how I love my grandmother.

(TRACY *goes up front of sofa.*)

DEXTER. Uncle Willie's around in the pantry, doing weird and wonderful things. Just say I said, One of the same.

MIKE. *(Moves toward the porch and below table to Left 1)* Is it all right if I say Two?

DEXTER. That's between you and your grandmother. (MIKE *exits Left 1.*) —And find Liz!

(TRACY *sits armchair Right Center*. DEXTER *goes to* TRACY *with the drink*) Doctor's orders, Tray.

TRACY. What is it?

DEXTER. Just the juice of a few flowers.

TRACY. *(Takes the glass and looks at it. Drinks)* Peppermint—

DEXTER. —White.—And one other simple ingredient. It's called a stinger. It removes the sting.

TRACY. *(Sets the glass down on coffee table and looks away)* Oh, Dext—don't say that!

DEXTER. Why not, Tray?

TRACY. —Nothing will—nothing ever can. *(Rises)* Oh, Dexter—I've done the most terrible thing to you!

DEXTER. *(At her chair. After a moment)* To *me*, did you say? (TRACY *nods vigorously*) I doubt that, Red. I doubt it very much.

TRACY. You don't know, you don't know!

DEXTER. Well, maybe I shouldn't.

TRACY. You've got to—you must! I couldn't stand it, if you didn't! Oh, Dext—what am I going to do?

DEXTER. —But why to *me*, darling? (TRACY *looks at him*) Where do I come into it any more? *(Still* TRACY *looks)* Aren't you confusing me with someone else?—A fellow named Kittredge, or something?

TRACY. *(Front of armchair Right Center)* George—

DEXTER. That's right; George Kittredge. A splendid chap—very high morals—very broad shoulders.—

TRACY. *(Crossing to the telephone Left)* I've got to tell him.

DEXTER. *(Follows her)* Tell him what?

TRACY. I've got to tell him. *(Dials a number.)*

DEXTER. *(Goes above table to Right of her)* But if he's got any brain at all, he'll have realized by this time what a fool he made of himself, when he—

TRACY. —When he what? *(To the telephone.* DEXTER *goes up Center and over to Right, back of sofa)* Hello? Hello, George—this is Tracy. Look—I don't care whether it's bad luck or not, but I've got to see you for a minute before the wedding.—What, *what* note? I didn't get any note.—When? Well, why didn't someone tell me?—Right. Come on the run. *(Replaces the telephone, goes up to mantel to a wall-bell and rings it)* He sent a note over at ten o'clock.

DEXTER. I told you he'd come to his senses.

TRACY. Was—was he here, too?

DEXTER. Sure.

TRACY. *(Crossing down Center)* My God—why didn't you sell tickets?

DEXTER. *(Crossing over Right, gets glass from table; gives it to her)* Finish your drink.

TRACY. *(Taking drink)* Will it help?

DEXTER. There's always the hope.

(EDWARD *comes into the hall doorway, Right 2.)*

EDWARD. You rang, Miss?

TRACY. *(Crossing to Center above* DEXTER*)* Isn't there a note for me from Mr. Kittredge somewhere?

(DEXTER *gets Left Center.)*

EDWARD. I believe it was put on the hall table upstairs. Mrs. Lord said not to disturb you.

TRACY. I'd like to have it, if I may.

EDWARD. Very well, Miss. *(Exits Right 2.)*

TRACY. *(Finishes her drink. Right Center. Gives* DEXTER *glass)* Say something, Dext—anything.

DEXTER. No—you do.

TRACY. Oh, Dext—I'm wicked! *(Crossing Left)* I'm such an unholy mess of a girl.

DEXTER. That's no good. That's not even conversation.

TRACY. But never in all my life—not if I live to be one hundred—will I ever forget the way you tried to—to stand me on my feet again this morning.

DEXTER. *(Crossing front of table Left)* You—you're in grand shape. Tell me: what did you think of my wedding present? I like my presents at least to be acknowledged.

TRACY. *(Turns to him)* It was beautiful and sweet, Dext.

DEXTER. She was quite a boat, the "True Love."

TRACY. Was, and is.

DEXTER. She had the same initials as yours—did you ever realize that?

TRACY. No, I never did. *(Sits in chair Left of table.)*

DEXTER. *(Puts glass down)* Nor did I, till I last saw her.—Funny we missed it. My, she was yare. *(Leans over table to her.)*

TRACY. She was yare, all right. *(A moment)* I wasn't, was I?

DEXTER. Wasn't what?

TRACY. Yare.

DEXTER. *(Laughs shortly)* Not very. *(Sits in chair Right of table)* —You were good at the brightwork, though. I'll never forget you down on your knees on the deck every morning, with your little can of polish.

TRACY. I wouldn't let even you help, would I?

DEXTER. Not even me.

TRACY. I made her shine.—Where is she now?

DEXTER. In the yard at Seven Hundred Acre, getting gone over. I'm going to sell her to Ruff Watriss at Oyster Bay.

TRACY. You're going to sell the "True Love"?

DEXTER. Why not?

TRACY. For money?

DEXTER. He wired an offer yesterday.

TRACY. —To *that* fat old rum-pot?

DEXTER. What the hell does it matter?

TRACY. She's too clean, she's too yare.

DEXTER. I know—but when you're through with a boat, you're— *(Looks at her)* That is, of course, unless *you* want her. (TRACY *is silent*) Of course she's good for nothing but racing—and only really comfortable for two people—and not so damned so, for them. So I naturally thought—. But of course, if *you* should want her—

TRACY. No—I don't want her.

DEXTER. I'm going to design another for myself, along a little more practical lines.

TRACY. Are you?

DEXTER. I started on the drawings a couple of weeks ago.

TRACY. What will you call her?

DEXTER. I thought the "True Love II."— What do you think?

TRACY. *(After a moment)* Dexter, if you call any boat that, I promise you I'll blow you and it right out of the water! *(Rises.)*

DEXTER. I know it's not very imaginative, but— *(Rises.)*

TRACY. *(Crossing in to Right Center to armchair)* Just try it, that's all! *(Moves away from him)* I'll tell you what you can call it, if you like—

DEXTER. What?

TRACY. In fond remembrance of me—

DEXTER. What?

TRACY. The "Easy Virtue."

DEXTER. *(Crossing to her Right)* Tray, I'll be damned if I'll have you thinking such things of yourself!

TRACY. What would you like me to think?

DEXTER. I don't know. But I do know that virtue, so-called, is no matter of a single misstep or two.

TRACY. You don't think so?

DEXTER. I know so. It's something inherent, it's something regardless of anything.

TRACY. Like fun it is.

DEXTER. You're wrong. The occasional misdeeds are often as good for a person as—as the more persistent virtues.—That is, if the person is there. Maybe you haven't committed enough, Tray. Maybe this is your coming-of-age.

TRACY. *(Crossing to Left)* I don't know.—Oh, I don't know anything any more!

DEXTER. That sounds very hopeful. That's just fine, Tray.

(Enter EDWARD, Right 2, with note on salver.)

TRACY. *(Over Left)* Oh, be still, you! *(Turns. EDWARD comes back to table Left with note and gives it to her)* Thanks, Edward.

EDWARD. They are practically all in, Miss—and quite a number standing in the back. (MIKE *and* LIZ *come in Left 2)* All our best wishes, Miss.

(LIZ crosses down Left, back of Left Center armchair. MIKE back of Left table.)

TRACY. Thanks, Edward. Thanks, very much.

LIZ. —And all ours, Tracy.

(EDWARD goes up Right Center.)

TRACY. Thank you, thank everybody. *(Opens note.)*

(SANDY rushes in Right 2 and goes to her, Left. EDWARD goes out Right 2.)

SANDY. Tray—he's here! He's arrived!

TRACY. Who has?

SANDY. Kidd—Sidney Kidd.

TRACY. What for? What does *he* want?

LIZ. May I scream?

MIKE. What the—!

TRACY. Oh, now I remember.

SANDY. Well, I should hope you would. I haven't been to bed at all. I gave him the profile. He's reading it now. I couldn't stand the suspense, so I—

MIKE. Profile, did you say? What profile?

SANDY. *(Crossing to* MIKE—*back of table)* The Kidd himself, complete with photographs. Do you want to see a copy?

MIKE. Holy Saint Rose of South Bend!

SANDY. —Offered in exchange for yours of us. I've told him what a help you'd both been to me.

LIZ. *(Left)* I don't think you'll find it so hard to resign now, Mike. Me neither.

MIKE. *(Left back of table)* That's all right with me.

LIZ. Belts will be worn tighter this winter.

SANDY. I'll see how he's bearing up. *(Moves up to door Right 2.* DR. PARSONS *enters Right 2)* Good morning, Doctor Parsons. How's everything?

DR. PARSONS. Where is your sister? *(Goes down back of sofa.* SANDY *points to her and goes out Right 2.* TRACY *is reading the note)* Tracy? Tracy!

TRACY. *(Looks up, startled)* Yes?

(He smiles, and beckons engagingly.)

DEXTER. *(Upstage corner of sofa)* One minute, Doctor Parsons, Mr. Kittredge is on his way.

(DR. PARSONS *smiles again, and goes out into the living room, Right 1.)*

DEXTER. *(Turns to* TRACY*)* I'm afraid it's the deadline, Tracy.

TRACY. *(Center)* So is this. Listen— "My dear Tracy: Your conduct last night was so shocking to my ideals of womanhood, that my attitude toward you and the prospects of a happy and useful life together has changed materially. Your, to me, totally unexpected breach of common decency, not to mention the moral aspect—"

GEORGE. *(Comes in from the porch, Left 1)* Tracy!

TRACY. Hello, George.

GEORGE. Tracy—all these people! *(Goes Center.)*

TRACY. It's only a letter from a friend. They're my friends, too. "—not to mention the moral aspect, certainly entitles me to a full explanation, before going through with our proposed marriage. In the light of day, I am sure that you will agree with me. Otherwise, with profound regrets and all best wishes, yours very sincerely—" *(Folds the note and returns it to its envelope)* Yes, George, I quite agree with you—in the light of day or the dark of night, for richer, for poorer, for better, for worse, in sickness, and in health—and thank you so very much for your good wishes at this time.

GEORGE. *(Center)* That's all you've got to say?

TRACY. *(Right Center)* What else? I wish for your sake, as well as mine, I had an explanation. But unfortunately I've none. You'd better just say "good riddance," George.

GEORGE. It isn't easy, you know.

TRACY. I don't see why.

LIZ. *(Crossing down Left to MIKE)* Say something, Stupid.

MIKE. *(Down Left in front of chair)* Wait a minute.

GEORGE. You'll grant I had a right to be angry, and very angry.

TRACY. You certainly had, you certainly have.

GEORGE. "For your sake, as well," you said—

TRACY. Yes—it would be nice to know.

LIZ. *(To* MIKE*)* Will you say something?

MIKE. Wait! *(Goes in Left Center, front of table.)*

LIZ. What for?

MIKE. Enough rope.

GEORGE. —On the very eve of your wedding, an affair with another man—

TRACY. I told you I agreed, George— *(Crossing Left below him to near chair Left Center)* and I tell you again, good riddance to me.

GEORGE. That's for me to decide.

TRACY. Well, I wish you would a—a—little more quickly.

MIKE. Look, Kittredge—

TRACY. If there was some way to make you see that—that regardless of it—or even because of it,— I'm—somehow I feel more of a person, George.

GEORGE. That's a little difficult to understand.

TRACY. Yes, I can see that it would be. *(Sits Left Center armchair.)*

DEXTER. Not necessarily.

GEORGE. You keep out of it!

DEXTER. You forget: I am out of it. *(Sits on sofa.)*

MIKE. *(Front of tablel Left)* Kittredge, it just might interest you to know that the so-called "affair" consisted of exactly two kisses and one rather late swim.

TRACY. Thanks, Mike, but there's no need to—

MIKE. *(To* TRACY*)* All of which I thoroughly enjoyed, and the memory of which I wouldn't part with for anything.

TRACY. It's no use, Mike.

MIKE. —After which, I accompanied her to her room, deposited her on her bed, and promptly returned to you two on the porch—as you will doubtless remember.

DEXTER. Doubtless without a doubt.

GEORGE. You mean to say that was all there was to it?

MIKE. I do.

(GEORGE *ponders.*)

TRACY. *(Is looking at* MIKE *in astonishment. Suddenly she rises and demands of him)* Why? Was I so damned unattractive—so distant, so forbidding or something, that—?

GEORGE. This is fine talk, too!

TRACY. I'm asking a question!

MIKE. *(Softens)* You were extremely attractive —and as for distant and forbidding, on the contrary. But you were also somewhat the worse—or the better—for wine, and there are rules about that, damn it.

TRACY. Thank you, Mike. I think men are wonderful.

LIZ. *(Down Left)* The little dears.

GEORGE. *(Center)* Well, that's a relief, I'll admit. Still—

TRACY. *(Turns to Center)* Why? Where's the difference? If my wonderful, marvelous, beautiful virtue is still intact, it's no thanks to me, I assure you.

GEORGE. I don't think—

TRACY. —It's purely by courtesy of the gentleman from South Bend.

LIZ. Local papers, please copy.

GEORGE. I fail to see the humor in this situation, Miss Imbrie.

LIZ. I appreciate that. It was a little hard for me too, at first—

TRACY. Oh, Liz— *(Goes down Left to* LIZ.*)*

LIZ. It's all right, Tracy. We all go a little haywire at times—and if we don't, maybe we ought to.

TRACY. Liz.

LIZ. You see, Mr. Kittredge, it wasn't Tracy at all. It was another girl: a Miss Pommery, '26.

GEORGE. You'd had too much to drink—

TRACY. *(Crossing to him Center)* That seems to be the consensus of opinion.

GEORGE. Will you promise me never to touch the stuff again?

TRACY. *(Looks at him; speaks slowly)* No, George, I don't believe I will. There are certain things about that other girl I rather like.

GEORGE. But a man expects his wife to—

TRACY. —To behave herself. Naturally.

DEXTER. To behave herself naturally. (GEORGE *glances)* Sorry.

GEORGE. *(To* TRACY*)* But if it hadn't been for the drink last night, all this might not have happened.

TRACY. But apparently nothing did. What made you think it had?

GEORGE. It didn't take much imagination, I can tell you that.

TRACY. Not much, perhaps—but just of a certain kind.

GEORGE. It seems *you* didn't think any too well of yourself.

TRACY. That's the odd thing, George: *(Crossing Right in front of armchair)* somehow I'd have hoped you'd think better of me than I did.

GEORGE. I'm not going to quibble, Tracy: all the evidence was there.

TRACY. And I was guilty straight off—that is, until I was proved innocent.

GEORGE. Well?

DEXTER. Downright un-American, if you ask me.

GEORGE. No one is asking you!

SANDY. *(Comes in Right 2, consternation on his face. Remains on doorstep)* Listen—he's read it— and holy cats, guess what?

LIZ. What?

SANDY. He loves it! He says it's brilliant— **He** wants it for *Destiny!*

MIKE. I give up.

GEORGE. Who wants what?

LIZ. Sidney Kidd; Sidney Kidd.

GEORGE. *(Pleased and astonished)* Sidney Kidd is here himself?!

SANDY. Big as life, and twice as handsome. Boy, is this wedding a National affair now! *(Exits Right 2.)*

GEORGE. *(After a moment)* It's extremely kind and thoughtful of him. *(Another moment. Then)* Come on, Tracy—it must be late. Let's let bygones be bygones—what do you say?

TRACY. *(Right Center)* Yes—and goodbye, George.

GEORGE. I don't understand you.

TRACY. Please—goodbye.

GEORGE. *(Center)* But what on earth—?

LIZ. I imagine she means that your explanation is inadequate.

GEORGE. Look here, Tracy—

TRACY. You're too good for me, George. You're a hundred times too good.

GEORGE. I never said I—

TRACY. And I'd make you most unhappy, most— *(Crosses Right corner of sofa)* That is, I'd do my best to.

GEORGE. Well, if that's the way you want it—

TRACY. That's the way it is.

GEORGE. *(Looks at her)* All right. Possibly it's just as well. *(Starts up Right.)*

DEXTER. I thought you'd eventually think so.

GEORGE. *(Confronts him from back of sofa)* I've got a feeling you've had more to do with this than anyone.

DEXTER. A novel and interesting idea, I'm sure.

GEORGE. You and your whole rotten class.

DEXTER. Oh, class my—! *(But he stops himself.)*

MIKE. *(Crossing in Center. Sits on arm of chair Left Center)* Funny—I heard a truck-driver say that yesterday—only with a short "a."

GEORGE. Listen, you're all on your way out—the lot of you—and don't think you aren't.—Yes, and good riddance. *(He goes out Right 2.)*

MIKE. There goes George—

(ORCHESTRA plays "Oh Promise Me.")

TRACY. *(Rushes over to door Right 1; looks off)* Oh, my sainted aunt—that welter of faces! *(Closes door, and returns to up Center. MAY, the housemaid, appears Right 2 with TRACY's hat and gloves)* What in the name of all that's holy am I to do?

MAY. *(Crossing to Center)* You forgot your hat, Miss Tracy. *(Gives them to her and exits Right 2.)*

TRACY. Oh, God— Oh, dear God—have mercy on Tracy!

MIKE. *(Rises)* Tracy—

TRACY. Yes, Mike?

MIKE. *(Crossing in Center to TRACY)* Forget the license!

TRACY. License?

DEXTER. I've got an old one here, that we never used, Maryland being quicker—

MIKE. Forget it! *(To TRACY)* Old Parson Parsons —he's never seen Kittredge, has he? Nor have most of the others. I got you into this, I'll get you out.— Will you marry me, Tracy?

TRACY. *(A pause)* No, Mike.—Thanks, but no. *(Goes Left. Puts hat in chair Left Center.)*

MIKE. But listen, I've never asked a girl to marry me before in my life!—I've avoided it!—You've got me all confused—why not—?

TRACY. *(Left Center)* —Because I don't think Liz would like it—and I'm not sure that you would—

and I'm even a little doubtful about myself. But—I'm beholden to you, Mike, I'm most beholden.

MIKE. *(Center)* They're in there! They're waiting!

LIZ. *(Front of Left chair)* Don't get too conventional all at once, will you?—There'll be a reaction.

MIKE. Liz— *(Goes Left.)*

LIZ. I count on you sustaining the mood.

DEXTER. *(Rising)* It'll be all right, Tracy: you've been got out of jams before.

TRACY. *(Between corner of sofa and Right armchair)* Been *got out* of them, did you say?

DEXTER. That's what I said, Tracy. Don't worry, (MARGARET *and* SETH *enter from Right 2)* you always are. *(Rises; goes up corner of sofa.)*

MARGARET. *(At upper corner of sofa)* Tracy, we met George in the hall—it's all right, dear, your father will make a very simple announcement.

SETH. *(Back of Right armchair)* Is there anything special you want me to say?

TRACY. No! I'll say it, whatever it is.—I won't be got out of anything more, thanks. *(She moves to the door Right 1.)*

(WILLIE *and* DINAH *enter Right 2. He goes Left Center. She goes to* SETH.)

UNCLE WILLIE. What's alack? What's amiss?

MARGARET. *(Crossing to* SETH*)* Oh, this just can't be happening—it can't.

(TRACY *reaches door Right 1.* MIKE *crosses Right to sofa beside* DEXTER.)

TRACY. *(Having thrown the doors open)* I'm—I'm—hello! Good morning.—I'm—that is to say—I'm terribly sorry to have kept you waiting, but—but there's been a little hitch in the proceedings. I've made a terrible fool of myself—which isn't unusual —and my fiancé—my fiancé— *(She stops.)*

MARGARET. Seth!

SETH. Wait, my dear.

TRACY. —my fiancé, that was, that is—he thinks we'd better call it a day, and I quite agree with him. —Dexter—Dexter—what the hell next?

DEXTER. "Two years ago you were invited to a wedding in this house and I did you out of it by eloping to Maryland—" *(Rushes over to MARGARET.)*

TRACY. "Two years ago you were invited to a wedding in this house and I did you out of it by eloping to Maryland—" Dexter, Dexter, where are you?

DEXTER. *(To MARGARET)* May I? Just as a loan? *(Takes ring from her finger; goes to MIKE)* Here, put this in your vest pocket.

MIKE. But I haven't got a vest.

DEXTER. Then hold it in your hand. *(Rejoins TRACY.)*

DEXTER. *(To TRACY)* "Which was very bad manners—"

TRACY. "Which was very bad manners—"

DEXTER. "But I hope to make it up to you by going through with it now, as originally planned."

TRACY. "But I hope to make it up to you by—by going—" —by going beautifully through with it now—as originally and —most beautifully— planned. Because there's something awfully nice about a wedding—I don't know—they're gay,

DEXTER. *(Rushes to MIKE)* I'd like you to be my best man, if you will, because I think you're one hell of a guy, Mike.

MIKE. I'd be honored. C. K.

UNCLE WILLIE. Ladies, follow me: no rushing, please.

and attractive—and I've   (LIZ *and* MARGARET *go*
always wanted one—   *out with him, Right 2.*
                            WILLIE *goes last.)*

DEXTER. "So if you'll just keep your seats a minute—"

TRACY. "So if you'll just keep your seats a minute—"

DEXTER. That's all.

TRACY. "That's all!" *(MURMURS off Right 1. And she closes the living room doors; turns to* DEXTER, *down Right)* Dexter—are you sure?

DEXTER. Not in the least; but I'll risk it—will you?

TRACY. You bet!—And you didn't do it just to soften the blow?   *(WARN Curtain.)*

DEXTER. No, Tray.

TRACY. Nor to save my face?

DEXTER. It's a nice little face.

TRACY. Oh—I'll be yare now—I'll promise to be yare!

DEXTER. Be whatever you like, you're my Redhead.—All set?

TRACY. All set!—Oh, how did this ever happen? *(Running Left Center—gets hat from chair, goes Left, looking in mirror, puts on hat.)*

SETH. Don't inquire.— Go on, Dinah: tell Mr. Dutton to start the music.

DINAH. *(Going up)* I did it—I did it all! *(Exits Right 2.)*

(DEXTER *and* MIKE *go to door Right 2.)*

SETH. Daughter—

TRACY. *(Crossing over to* SETH, *Center)* I love you, Father.

SETH. And I love you, daughter.

TRACY. Never in my life have I been so full of love before—

(MUSIC: "Wedding March.")

DEXTER. See you soon, Red!

TRACY. See you soon, Dext! (DEXTER *and* MIKE *exit Right 2)* How do I look?

SETH. Like a queen—like a goddess.

TRACY. Do you know how I feel?

SETH. How?

TRACY. Like a human—like a human being!

SETH. —And is that all right?

TRACY. *(She takes his arm. They slowly start down Right Center towards door Right 1)* All right? Oh, Father, it's Heaven!

(SWELL MUSIC for Curtain.)

CURTAIN

THE PHILADELPHIA STORY

THE SCENES

ACT ONE AND THREE

The Living Room.

The set is 16′ high, with a 34′ opening. The back wall is 30′ across.

The Left wall is 15′ deep with two French windows opening out onto a porch. This porch is 18″ high with a step of 8″ in front of each window leading out onto it. Between these two windows is a 3′ space to allow for furniture.

The Right wall, starting downstage, is an 8′ flat in which is centered a double door, each door 3′. A jog, on stage, of 4′, then a 5′ 9″ flat going up, to join the back flat. In the 5′ 9″ flat is centered a single door. An 18″ platform is offstage against this door and an 8″ step in front of it.

In the back flat (not centered because of the 4′ jog over Right) is a mantelpiece 5′ high and 8′ long. This is centered in the room.

The backing out Right is a library, double wing. Up Right a double wing hall. The out Left porch has a grill column and wainscoting treatment with green bushes backing it.

THE SCENES

ACT TWO

The Porch

From Left stage to over Right, going 30', is a large platform 18" high. In front of this is an 8" step, 18' long. The platform is 10' deep. In the back wall are two French windows (supposed to be the same windows of Act I) with the same width of space between them. The Left wall is a 10' flat with a large single arch centered. The Right wall is of columns, downstage and up. In front, at each end of the platform is a like column with a trellis grillwork at top joining all columns.

The backing for the French windows is a painted room-backing—supposed to be a wall of Act I room. 18' high and 30' long.

The Left room is also a platform 18" high, level with the porch, while the back room is reached by a down-step from the porch.

The porch continues, over Right, stage floor level, with columns down front and two upstage, with the grill at top joining them. Green bushes back between the columns and a blue cyclorama backs the entire Right stage.

THE PHILADELPHIA STORY

FURNITURE AND DRESSING PLOT

A painted ground cloth covers the entire room.

Down Right against the four-foot jog is a bookcase cabinet, filled with books. On top of the case is a pair of figures and a vase of pink roses. On the wall above is a good portrait of an ancestor, male.

A fireside chair the Right side of mantel. A small green silk stool in front of it and a gold brocade fireside chair the other side of said mantel. Fire screen and dogs with logs complete it.

On top of mantel a small clock, a pair of marble figures and a pair of crystal candlesticks. (Ornate) A large portrait of a man (supposed to be Gilbert Stuart) is centered over the mantel, with one small painted gold-framed mirror picture on either side of the portrait.

A foot from the mantel, going Right stage, is a floor whatnot, its shelves filled with bric-a-brac. At Left of mantel is a grand piano in the upper Left corner of the room. On this piano is an odd assortment of framed signed photographs, a large crock of large roses, all colors, sheet music and a pair of very large gold or bronzed figures about 16" high.

Over the piano on the upper Left wall is a very large framed picture. An outdoor farm picture.

A small French desk is between the wall windows Left. On this desk is a telephone, a writing set, many letters, vase of flowers, a figurine and over it on the wall is a gilt mirror.

A desk chair.

Left Center is a table 24″ by 36″ and on it a vase of flowers, magazine, smoking tray; lighter and cigarettes in box. A large comfortable chair either side of this table.

Over Right Center is a sofa with a coffee table fronting it. Cushions on the sofa; ash tray and cigarettes and lighter on the table. Also a book or two. An armchair near the upstage end of this sofa.

Chintz draperies with silk green over-drapes at the two French windows.

Off Right 1 is a supposed parlor. Backing the double doors is a commode table with large bowl of flowers. On the two walls, large paintings.

Two crystal wall brackets are on either side of the large mantel portrait, and a large crystal chandelier hangs centered in the ceiling.

THE PHILADELPHIA STORY

COSTUME PLOT

ACT ONE

TRACY LORD:
> First—Cream-colored silk shorts, blouse, skirt and sport slippers.
> Second—Crepe silk checked blue and white dress; white hair ribbon bow, red sports slippers.

LIZ IMBRIE:
> Grey crepe silk suit, tan shoes and stockings, white blouse.

MARGARET LORD:
> Daytime (magenta) silk crepe dress, neutral stockings, tan shoes.

DINAH LORD:
> First—Day dress of gingham, white socks, sport shoes.
> Second—Clean day dress, white socks and sport shoes (the same ones).

MIKE CONNOR:
> Light brown sport suit; tan shoes, white shirt and green tie.

DEXTER HAVEN:
> Grey flannel slacks, darker grey jacket, brown shoes, natural linen shirt, tie.

SANDY LORD:
> Grey flannel slacks, checked sport coat, tan shoes, blue shirt. red tie.

UNCLE WILLIE:
Checked trousers, sport jacket (dark grey), white shoes and socks, tan shirt and tie, colored handkerchief, red carnation.

SETH LORD:
Street suit; carries topcoat and hat.

EDWARD (Footman):
Oxford grey coat, striped trousers, black shoes and socks, dress shirt, wing collar, black four-in-hand tie.

THOMAS (Butler):
Dress coat, black vest, grey trousers, black shoes and socks, dress shirt, wing collar, black string tie.

GEORGE KITTREDGE:
Grey double-breasted suit, soft shirt, tan shoes, and socks.

ACT TWO—SCENE I

TRACY LORD:
White pleated evening gown, bright red lounging robe, white evening shoes.

LIZ:
First — Grey skirt (from Act I), lavender sweater, same shoes and stockings, white blouse (from Act I).
Second—Black silk evening gown, black shoes, corsage, black handkerchief.

MARGARET:
Grey and chartreuse chiffon evening gown, grey slippers and stockings, brooch.

DINAH:
First—Yellow sport jersey shirt (soiled), washed-out blue dungarees, soiled sport shoes.
Second—Evening dress, shoes, stockings, hair ribbon.

ELSIE (Maid):
> Black silk dress, shoes and stockings, white apron and cap, collar and cuffs.

MIKE: Dinner clothes.

SANDY:
> First—Same as Act One.
> Second—Dinner clothes.

SETH:
> First—White trousers, shoes, shirt, blue sport jacket.
> Second—Dinner clothes.

GEORGE: Same as Act I.

DEXTER: Same as Act I.

WILLIE: Same as Act I plus pipe.

THOMAS: Evening clothes with brass buttons.

EDWARD: Black trousers, tail coat, yellow and black striped vest, black shoes, white dress shirt, collar and tie from Act I.

SCENE TWO

TRACY:
> First—Same as Scene I without red robe.
> Second—Bathrobe (TERRY).

SANDY: Dinner clothes.

MIKE:
> First—Dinner trousers, shirt, shoes, tie, gray sport coat.
> Second—White terry bathrobe—sandals.

DEXTER: Grey flannels from Act One; tan crew-necked sweater, tan sport crepe shoes, neck scarf.

GEORGE: Dinner clothes.

MAC (Watchman): Odd trousers, suede jacket, slouch hat, tan shoes, pipe.

ACT THREE

TRACY LORD: Pink tulle wedding dress, pink slip-

pers; later adds: hat (pink), gloves and flowered muff.

DINAH LORD:

First—Dungaree outfit from Scene I of Act II
but with clean shirt.

Second—Blue chiffon wedding dress, blue slippers, corsage, hair ribbon.

MARGARET: Green morning dress for wedding,
green slippers, neutral stockings.

LIZ: Brown silk print dress, same shoes and stockings from Act I. Carries white hat; gloves and
bag.

MAY (Maid): Black silk dress, white cap and collar, apron. Black shoes and stockings.

DR. PARSONS (Episcopal Minister): Long black
robe, white lace surplice, white stole, black
shoes.

THOMAS: Same as Act I.

EDWARD: Same as Act I.

MIKE: Blue street suit, black shoes and socks, white
shirt and blue tie.

SETH: Morning jacket, striped trousers.

WILLIE: Morning clothes, white flower.

SANDY: Morning clothes.

GEORGE: Blue suit, soft white shirt, black shoes, tie.

DEXTER: Grey gabardine suit, white shirt, striped
tie, tan shoes.

THE PHILADELPHIA STORY

PROPERTY PLOT

ACT ONE

On stage, Down Right:
Sofa with two cushions.
Coffee table with magazine, ashtray, lighter, silver cigarette box (full), two books.
Pink satin armchair.
Cabinet bookcase with books on shelves, vase flowers on top, pair figures on top.

Up Right:
Break-front cabinet with many figures on shelves; center shelf, pewter urn with green leaves, small gold-framed pictures, low bowl flowers.

At Fireplace, Center:
Fireside chair and cushion, small green silk bench, fireside chair (two gift-boxes on chair), fireplace screen, dogs, logs.

On Mantel, Center:
Small marble clock, two small figures. Each end: A large crystal candlestick, cardboard gift box (6"x9").

Un Left Center: Floor standing what-not with **five** shelves filled with bric-a-brac.

Up Left: Period grand piano and bench. On piano: Sheet music, large crock of large roses, all col- **ors; three** framed photographs, pair bronze statue candlesticks (large), three various-sized gift-boxes, opened, showing tissue paper so that the contents cannot be seen.

Over against Left Wall:

Small French desk with gilt mirror over it.
China inkstand.
Framed photo.
Figure.
Stationery.
French telephone.
Four gift-boxes opened with tissue and wedding presents showing.
Desk chair.

Over Left:

Library table with vase flowers, magazine, ash-tray and cigarette box, lighter, three letters (been mailed), pencil.
Armchair.
Armchair with black writing-pad complete, oblong box of addressed envelopes.

Side Props—Off Right:

Tray with decanter of sherry.
8 small napkins.
8 sherry glasses.
Small white box with horse puzzle. This is about 6"x6" and flat.
Roll of parchment about 30"x15", to represent seating arrangement of dinner guests.
Large box, flat, holding 3 smaller ones of gifts. One supposed to be a Dutch muffin-ear (not seen). One with game-shears (seen). One with 2 small odd-colored boxes.
Salver.
Contax camera with shoulder strap.

ACT TWO (Both I and II Scenes)

Over Right: Green wicker settee with one cushion.

Up Right: One floor stand of geraniums—narrow floor pad.

Up Right on Platform: Stand of geraniums.

Over Left on Platform: Stand of geraniums.

Center Stage: Round table with armchair either side of it.

  On Table: 3 sheets of narrow writing paper, pencil, yellow tray with 3 glasses, pitcher of orange juice.

Over Left: Wicker chaise-longue with cushion—narrow floor-pad.

Offstage Right:

  Tray with 1 bottle Champagne, opened and 2/3 full of Celery Tonic.

  Pitcher of cocktails, with spoon.

  4 cocktail glasses.

  4 champagne glasses.

  6 small napkins.

  Tray with pitcher of milk, milk glass.

  2 Pomery bottles, one opened and 2/3 full Celery Tonic.

  3 champagne glasses.

  Real red rose.

On Stage Left:

  Wrapped in tissue, a small framed sailboat picture.

  Small volume (good-looking).

  Salver with note.

  6 photographs.

Offstage Center:

  Telephone.

  Table, chair, piano from Act I.

ACT THREE

Same furniture as in Act I.
Flowers.

Add:

2 vases roses to cabinet down Right.

3 vases offstage Right.

1 to table Left.

1 to piano; put Act I piano vase off Right. Act I off Right vase to piano.

2 to desk.

Side Props, off Left:

Cocktail (stinger).

Off Right:

Salver with written letter (from GEORGE).

Minister's prayer-book.

Manuscript (typed).

Man's wrist watch.

TRACY's hat, gloves, flowered muff.

Act I and III windows have cretonne drapes, green silk over-drapes.

Act II brown silk at door Left, tan sateen lining with cretonne edging at French doors.

Act I walls:

Man's portrait down Right.

Man's portrait over mantel.

Farm picture over Left.

Gilt mirror over Left side wall.

Pair gild frames back wall.

Pair paintings off Right.

Pair crystal wall brackets back wall.

THE PHILADELPHIA STORY

PUBLICITY THROUGH YOUR LOCAL PAPERS

The press can be an immense help in giving publicity to your productions. In the belief that the best reviews from the New York and other large papers are always interesting to local audiences, and in order to assist you, we are printing below several excerpts from those reviews.

This gay and discerning comedy as produced by The Theatre Guild in New York City, starring Katharine Hepburn, has been one of the outstanding hits of 1939 and 1940, having enjoyed a solid year's run on Broadway before going on the road. New York City's drama critics were unanimous in their agreement that *The Philadelphia Story* presents Philip Barry at the very top of his form.

"A gay and sagacious comedy— When the Theatre Guild, Miss Hepburn, and Mr. Barry are in top form at the same time, all is for the best of all possible Broadways."—*New York Times.*

"It is pleasant to be able to report that Miss Katharine Hepburn, Mr. Philip Barry, and the Theatre Guild are all in good form once more— Lively and entertaining, written with all of Mr. Barry's graceful wit."—*New York Herald Tribune.*

"The *News* is on the cheering side this morning.

A pleasant comedy about pleasant, believable people, written in the Barry manner with dialogue that
is both smart and polished."—*New York News*.

"Alert and suave in his comedy and touched—
with tenderness."—*New York Sun*.

"The result is all to the theatre's good, and we can
report the season's most sparkling comedy. —the
best manipulator of light dialogue in the American
theatre."—*Philadelphia Ledger*.

"—one of the most delightful comedies seen here
in many a season. The dialogue is amusing, the char-
acterizations at their most satiric, touched with that
wistful cynicism and light-handed penetration which
is Barry at his suavest and best."—*Philadelphia
Record*.

"In addition to the sprightly and nippy writing,
which sets it off as a modern literary effort of no
little merit, it is merrily, moonily unconventional and
behaves like a strong hooker of bromo-seltzer. The
result is that he makes more direct hits with innu-
endo and subtlety than the others could with a self-
aiming shotgun."—*Philadelphia Daily News*.

"To put it in a palindrome, and for the enlighten-
ment of those who just must run as they read, the
verdict this morning is—it's a *wow*. —most sus-
tained, sparkling, sophisticated, completely captivat-
ing comedy. —nimble wit and impish twist of situation—"—*Philadelphia Inquirer*.

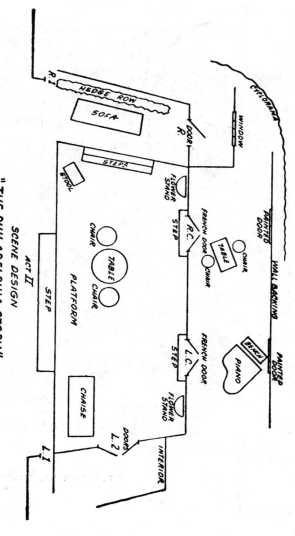

ACT II

SCENE DESIGN

"THE PHILADELPHIA STORY"

ACTS I & III
SCENE DESIGN
"THE PHILADELPHIA STORY"

PARLOR

CABINET

DOORS R1

BOOKCASE

HALL

DOOR R2

STEPS

SOFA

COFFEE TABLE

CHAIR

CABINET

CHAIR

FIRE PLACE

STOOL

CHAIR

CHAIR

TABLE

CHAIR

CHAIR

BENCH

PIANO

DESK

FRENCH DOOR L.2

FRENCH DOOR L.1

PORCH